Dear Ste

Thank
u
coming to celebrate the
Book launch, Lucy Ascham

Words Of The Wise

Words Of The Wise

The Divine Collective

Disclaimer
All information contained within this book is for informational and entertainment purposes only. Whilst we believe the information contained to be true at time of print, please check any facts, medical or otherwise before acting on any advice. The information contained within this book is not absolute and should not substitute for professional or medical advice. The Authors and Publishers disclaim liability for any adversity or loss incurred and any actions taken are the sole responsibility of the individual.

Published by The Divine Collective.

ISBN:
978 1 9196441 8 9 – Paperback
978 1 9196441 9 6 – E-book

Contents

Dedication

This book is dedicated to all those who are consciously creating a better world for themselves and, in turn, those around them. Those being a light in the dark and leading the way. To all those making the choice to heal and break generational curses. To those who persevere through dark nights, in anticipation of a brighter tomorrow. The hope-bringers, the light-healers.

This book is in your honour.

Foreword

Words of the Wise has been percolating for many years. It was a divine inspiration that had seeped into my conscious awareness, after spending some time reflecting on the gratitude I felt for the many wise souls that I had found myself in the company of in recent years.

I had been on my personal journey of awakening for some five or six years, and during that time I had reconnected to my passion of writing. It was something I used to immerse myself in as a teenager to let out my angst and unspoken trauma. It was a sweet release that helped me to take out what was inside and make sense of it outside of myself. Make it logical. Make it magical. It was both therapeutic and alchemy. Over time, I lost touch with this beautiful practice, in favour of wild nights out- which consequently led to addiction during my late teens and twenties. Not only did I lose touch with this nourishing practice of self-awareness and reflection, but I had also lost touch with me. I had found my life to be so outward facing that I had forgotten who I was and all of the things I loved. My talents, my passion, my individuality.

I felt lost. Alone. And desperate for something. Only I wasn't quite sure what that something was. I was about to discover, through a series of unfoldings, what that something was.

Firstly, I'd like to ask you to contemplate what the term 'awakening' means to you. I believe we all have our own personal interpretations, however the essence of each one will be the same. For me, it was a term that seemed abstract. I had heard it used in spiritual communities but never really grasped its true meaning. That was, until, those unfoldings brought me closer to universal truths, that- once realized, can't be unlearnt. It has now come to mean to me a conscious awareness of how everything is intrinsically linked. It's a startling awareness of the oneness of all things and how blessed we are to be having this earthly experience- in order to fully immerse ourselves in that oneness. The realization of what our senses are truly for and the knowing that this life is purposeful- on the deepest level.

Writing consequently became a massive part of my healing and a way in which to channel my wisdoms. The unfoldings I experienced are different from the ones you will experience, and from the others in this book. Each awakening is personal; each soul has different lessons to learn and blessings to give and receive.

My awakening took me into times of unshakeable darkness. It was spontaneous and I wasn't quite prepared for seeing the world with 'the light on'. It was as though I was woken abruptly with the light abrasively turned on whilst I was in the deepest slumber. I wasn't prepared to face that chaos and for seeing the world in this new light. I resisted, but this only made the process more unbearable. My whole reality changed in the space of a few moments- which caused me months of anguish and turmoil, as my fragile ego battled to defend the fading reality it had lived up until this point.

My first unfolding was surrender.

Surrendering to the process. To not really knowing what had happened, but to accepting that I had been profoundly and irrevocably changed. When I finally softened into this surrender, I found a sense of peace that I had never before experienced. I began to bask in this feeling and come to know it as unconditional love. I felt a deep, unreserved love- for myself, for others and for life. I began to see myself as a loving being and allowed love to flow into my life, in many, many different ways.

My second unfolding was recognising energy. Through the process of awakening, each and every one of my senses had become heightened. To a point it was almost painful. My empathy almost crippled me, as I looked around and actually felt into the suffering of others. My nervous system was in overdrive, as I was processing and healing my own trauma simultaneously. The sensations I would feel in my body were new to me. When something was coming up for healing, my body would physically react and this was something I hadn't experienced in the past. I would feel vibrations from within that would build, until I was visibly shaking. These processes used to scare me as I didn't understand what was happening, however, with the surrender into love, I learnt to embrace these spontaneous healings and know that I was being supported by love. On the other side of each healing episode, I would feel a sense of lightness, of ease, of clarity. Of space. It was the same feeling you get when you have cried (and often these healing episodes would include crying). The sense of calm after the storm. I began to recognise these experiences as neither positive or negative, but just as energy. A build-up of energy, stored within my body; that was opening up and raining down in order to transmute itself – free itself. It was surrendering, and reuniting itself with love.

The nature of humanity is to understand and search for truth and knowledge. We are intrigued by mystery and search for answers. And in doing so we like to quantify and put boxes around things. One thing we do this with is time. We make it linear to aid our comprehension. However, those on journeys of healing and awakening will tell you that this process is never linear. The same wounds may open up once we think we have 'healed' them. This just prompts us to drop deeper into understanding. Until we place love where the pain once was.

The more I leaned into my healing and the more space that freed up inside of me, the more I realised I was being blessed. With new connections, new opportunities, new realities. I was aligning with more pleasurable experiences and the things I desired began to manifest themselves in my life. This was a welcome unfolding. I was putting more focus onto the future; on to growth and adventure. This taught me about the potency of energy and the capacity we have as conscious beings to affect energy and manipulate it. When we do any action in alignment with love, and in surrender to it, it ultimately blesses our experience in ways we can only imagine.

I began to also recognise my heightened senses as a gift. They had always been there, however, they had been muted by my lack of conscious understanding and the numbing behaviours I had engaged in. Reuniting with these senses on a clean and pure level was nothing short of astonishing. It brought me into the present moment, as I would deliciate in the aroma of flowers, in the caress of silken sheets, in the warmth of the sun's rays. I felt more connected to my body and appreciative of the world around me. Unfolding into each moment with heartfelt gratitude and a sense of ease.

Connection– to myself and others, and also to the unseen has proved to be the greatest unfolding of all. I truly believe that we are all here to reflect back the love that we are for each other. To aid each other in the creation of beautiful life experiences. We are lock and keys for new earthly experiences and our job is to find those we resonate with, to unlock more divine potential. I still yearn for more connection sometimes, only now I recognise the longing. I can be conscious in the recognising and in the divine prompt to go inwards. To connect with myself first. To see what needs to be heard and acknowledged within me. Once I have given myself that space to come home, I can open up the doors and invite those I wish to share this beautiful and held space. Yearning is only the desire for reconnection.

"We are mirrors for each other,
So that we may know
In each lonely feeling
We are never alone" – Words Heal from Songs of the Soul, Siobhan Louise.

I believe that when we live from a place of conscious awareness, we allow wisdoms and intuition to gracefully be received. Women, in nature, are receptive and open. We often hear about 'women's intuition' and the wise women who were branded witches for their power and knowledge.

As you read through these pages you will discover the learnings and the wisdom these courageous women have uncovered. All have been on very different journeys; however, all tread the same holy grounds. All have journeyed through the same human emotions and felt the common threads of humanity that connect us all.

The writings in this book explore some of the underpinning themes of awakening, such as fear, healing, conscious awareness, unity and love. Our intention has been to demonstrate the similarities of each journey, despite the different circumstances. To illustrate to the reader that what they are experiencing on their own path is exactly as was intended and divinely orchestrated. To provide comfort in the knowledge that even though at times this path feels painful, there is a pure light guiding you. That you are not alone in this and that together we are raising the vibration of consciousness on this planet.

Each awakening is very different in essence, as each of us has a personal perspective of life, purpose and soul mission. Some of us are healers, with a divine purpose of guiding others in their healing. We must heal ourselves first and foremost. Some of us are here to bare light. But firstly, we must acquaint ourselves with darkness. Some of us are connectors, bringing together community and holding space for divine unions. But firstly, we must meet ourselves on the deepest level. Awakening is the quest for home. And the home is within us all.

We drift in and out of alignment. In and out of enlightenment. In and out of our humanness and in and out of our spiritual nature. And this is exactly what this earthly experience calls for. True peace comes with the acceptance of this, and the acknowledgement that human and soul can co-exist and thrive. Never denying any part of this symphony of life.

The Authors in this book have been called onto this sacred journey of sharing. To bring together this unique collection of words, which I believe will make a difference in the lives of so many. Gravitating together, to form a powerful coven, rich in knowledge and magic. Reflecting on the teachings, lessons and wisdom that have been bestowed upon them to be shared, to be witnessed and to be felt. It is in unity that we feel the oneness of love from which we all originate and have direct access to in any given moment. I believe that the words contained within this book will serve as a holy reminder of the sacredness inside of you. And your ability, at any given moment, to access and attune to the love from which you are made.

Siobhan's passion for writing and poetry began at a very young age. It was something that stayed with her throughout childhood and her teenage years to help her express her inner world. This later became part of her healing process and helped her to navigate her spiritual awakening.

She now guides others to use words as a way of healing, overcoming trauma and for self-expression. She is a certified Life/ Recovery Coach and Journal Therapist and is passionate about helping others to live a sensual and fully expressed life – in alignment with their highest self.

Her debut poetry anthology, Songs of the Soul became an Amazon Bestseller and her poem Internal Fight has been featured on BBC Upload.

She also helps people to share conscious messages with the world through her publishing platform The Divine Collective. She does this by helping others to bring to life the message they would like to share and publish their work in collaborations or as stand-alone authors.

Siobhan enjoys spending time with her son, stargazing, photography and walks in the wild.

You can find out more about her work here:

www.siobhanlouise.net

Sunrise

Awareness of love
Conscious light in the darkness
The sunrise of life.

Awake - The Insomniac Oracle's Diary

Swey Jitti

I lay awake
Thinking of the flesh -
To touch it
To Taste it
And to devour it

I lay awake
Thinking of the earth -
to feel it
to heal it
and to sink in it

I lay awake
Thinking of the beyond -
the deep dark
the height of light
and everything in between

I lay awake
Wandering the unknown
and the constant familiar
watching universes collide
and it's trail of enchanting chaos

I lay awake
Following the roots
of my divine core,
to paint my vision
to flow into my submission

I lay awake
And surrender
to the human I am
to the energy I hold
to the pasts and presents
that tell the tale
of my vivid soul.

Swey Jitti
https://linkpop.com/sweyjitti

Mulemba
Angelina Abel

Perspectives

I am aware of my surroundings! I move, I live. I deliver, yet my heart is pounding.
Warnings of my own being, alert mechanisms asking if I'm seeing,
The prism, the other dimension, perspectives and its true intentions,
Its effect and why the apprehension, examining and paying attention... To the path that I follow.

The path that was laid for me, sometimes impeding what I'm meant to be,
And through this vessel that is my body, guiding my destiny.
Creating roads and hidden pavements, routes with no equity filled with intensity,
Where a rebellious search of identity, wants to defy the tendency to freeze and just agree.

Transitioning from a state of fear to one of wholeness, it is clear.
(The pain not forgotten... Respect for my ancestor's blood in those fields of cotton!)
Snap your fingers and dare! You are ancestry and you have flair!
Taking pride on that crown Afro hair, sis you walk purposefully that's the reason they stare.
Your history has tragedy and trickery, impacting on how you perceive your own victories,
Yet it carries what can be seen from the periphery, that black girl magic and all its brilliancy.

"Dare for" I push forward! "Dare for" I drag that weight and still conquer!
"Dare for" I find the Dahomey within! "Dare for" I refuse to be boxed-in!
"Dare for" I look at how it has been! "Dare for" I shake the future and refuse to lock-in,
The strong, the vulnerable, the joyful and the susceptible, all which empower my melanin.

And it is through gratitude that I push fear apart
Taking over control of my life, of my soul, of my heart!

Detect

You are, you are, you are, what you are not!!!
Ideas, beliefs and imposed external interpretations,
Strongly contributing to how the I perceive the self and become an auto-bot.
Systems transpiring fertile imagination and clear manipulation by masses, judging who's worthy and who is not.

Therefore, reconnect!

Reconnect to the words of your elders, the wisdom of your roots which support your playfulness. Reconnect! Reconnect to the natural musicality of your body, which is not simply translated into entertaining movement, but is the essence of your SPIRIT! Reconnect! Listen, explore, discover and connect! To thinkers, writers, sisters and brothers that are searching for not only theirs but equally your truth.
Please connect.
Through a joyful smile as you cross paths! Through a kind word, through vulnerable words full of self-insights, to your community - an embrace to connect. To the song of your childhood sang in the language of your soul, denied to your grandparents but through which they self-liberate. Reconnect!

Through the spiritual sound of the drums, find your voice, expel your pain, chant your vision, set your intention and detect...you!

Nubian soul

Uncluttering your soul to break surrounding structures
Undoing all the harm that generations have brought to you
Unbinding from constrictions and becoming the conductor
Unveiling the self-love that is long due and that you are worthy of.

That love you find within is the steam through which you press and open doors.
Serving soundness to the brain and screaming readiness through your pores.
That feeling of expansion you deny and underserve,
Leaving you in tears and indisputably feeling hurt.

It is time baby! It is time to radiate and glow.
Through all that melanin, shea butter and cocoa that makes you so...
Much more tasty than a Bordeaux and exquisite than Art Nouveau.

You are worthy, you are queen, you are more than just a show.

A quintessence of your roots,
Rise to the challenge of your Nubian soul.
With Nefertiti and Nzinga before you,
Rise my queen, you weigh more than gold.

You embody energy and strength
With your sensitivities purposely withdrawn.
The world not understanding that it is your depth
That will change the narrative, above and beyond.

You are worthy! You are queen!
More than they claim can be seen.
You are a pillar! You are comfort!
You are the power that can intervene.

Identify that mission, your purpose, your ground to move.
Traverse your sea of options with your smile and natural groove.
Black woman, hear me out...there's some baggage to remove
Yet we plant the seeds, its fruits will grow and we only have ourselves to prove.

Shine!

Just seeking

I close my eyes and listen to the waves...
Perceiving in my own time what my heart and mind crave.
I curl, I hide, though stepping out is what the soul aims,
Raise an eyebrow, hand to forehead minimising the impact of life rays.

And...

Deep breaths as reality slowly hits, deep breaths as unearthing doesn't equal bliss.
Deep breaths as awareness can strike high, deep breaths to care for this soul of mine.
Deep breaths as tears roll down in despair, deep breaths as I know I also need to persevere.
Deep breaths to examine history and choices, deep breaths as there's also joy within these true voices.

(Sigh) In a cynical headshake agreement,
Activating this spiritual realm that is my treatment,
I roll my head around with a soft grasp and gasp...
(Pause)
Let silence prevail as it's a must.

The roll of my shoulders is clearly pursuing, a liberty of movement as healing is brewing.
Stretching up high connecting to my sun, we shall dance in prayer, a change has begun.
And I feel it in the whisper of my breath, a light of hope connects my soul to its depth,
And I choose to take charge of the process I follow, ensuring that its path is everything but hollow.

From my hair to my toe connectivity rewired, repeating emotions translated in fire.
I aspire, I become, I can and I am one!

In great kingdoms my origin started, communities of wardens where our children are guarded
Where aunties are our mums and neighbours are our aunties.
Where rituals are native and we're not chased by vigilantes.
Therefore, I rewire and rekindle my existence, claiming higher and higher that I come in peace, with my resistance.

My name is Angelina Abel, I am Angolan, raised in Portugal and the founder/artistic director of Mulembas d'Africa dance classes in Sheffield.

I am the founder of Mamawe Afro-Pean dance festival in Sheffield and producer of Rise – an 8 week development course for Black/ Mixed African women designed to empower, engage and encourage self-love and belief.

I am also the co-producer of COR/PO alongside film director Joao Paulo Simões. A project designed to incorporate a wide range of forms of artistic expression and where the body in motion evokes distant geographies.

Mulembas dance classes take place weekly, Wednesdays, 7pm to 8pm at Croft House Settlement and within these you can expect soulful movement interpretations fed by the Angolan culture in its varied dance forms. To find out more go to www.mulembasdafrica.com – contact: mulembasdafrica@gmail.com

Coming Home
Sharon L Franks

A journey of coming home.
Home to you.
Home to you, beyond the voices that have created stories from the past.
Home to you, the pure essence of wonder and light.
Home to you, child of the light, child of love.
Home to you, the beauty of each breath.
Home to you the all beauty, brilliance, expression of light and love.
Home to you, the brilliant you that radiates with divine love.
Home to you.
Home to you,
Home to you.
To be held within the radiant arms of love, the pure beauty of your soul,
Home to you.

Author Sharon L Franks
https://www.facebook.com/sharonfranksresultscoaching/

Upgrading my Inner Conversations

Arti Kakkad

"Every day in every way, I'm getting better and better"

- Emile Coué

There was a white, circular tower in the distance. It looked far away, but she got there in no time at all. There was a large door to get inside, with a golden knocker. She reached up to knock, but the door swung open. She went inside. There was an open lobby with a spiral staircase going upwards, and doors leading off the landings on each floor. She went up five flights of stairs, stepping into a corridor with a series of doors leading off it. She pushed open the first one. This room represented what would happen in 5 years if she made no changes at all. There was an untuned television in there, white noise crackling. The room was damp and dim. This was not the way to go. She closed the door behind her. The second door represented what would happen in 5 years if she made a few changes. She pushed the door open. Her relationship was peaceful. She had changed job. She had kids of her own. Things were chaotic but happy. She closed the door and moved along the corridor. The third door represented what would happen in 5 years if she stepped into her highest possible reality. It was very similar to the second room, with everything upgraded slightly - her business was thriving and her relationship deeper, with more vulnerability and intimacy. Things were happy here too. The next door represented a possible future life. She was singing and picking berries, vaguely aware of the other bodies moving through the forest with her doing the same, each companionably in their own world. Her mind was still. She didn't think too much. She was comfortable and accepting of where she was and who she was with.

She asked her higher self what she needed to do to achieve this future. 'Understand when people are acting out of fear and be patient with them. Learn how to change your own habitual thought patterns. Meditate more. Learn about emotions.'

That was the first therapy session that shifted me onto a path that changed my life. I'd had a really difficult couple of years. My score on the Holmes and Rahe stress scale, which gives you a stress score based on how many major life events you've faced in the last two years, was sky-high at more than 500. 'You have a high or very high risk of becoming ill in the near future.' I wasn't aware of this stress scale at the time and thought all these life events were just a normal part of being an adult. I wasn't even aware of what stress feels like in the body and what to do about it, so I thought I was going mad. I oscillated between angry and tearful, and I had no idea why. After starting and stopping counselling a few times because it didn't seem to be helping, my mental health was in a very poor state. I was so desperate for help that I began to look to things I'd never considered before for answers. On my search I came across something called future life progression. 'Ah', I thought, 'I can find out whether I am still living here with these people and in this job in 5 years. I mean, surely this can't be it?' I almost wanted permission to up and abandon my life for another.

I did a web search for future life progression and came across a therapist near my office who did it. I immediately made a booking. Never had I done so little research into something before partaking in it. Not knowing much about it and the desperation to get out of my mental tension helped my conscious mind take a back seat and allow the experience to unfold, as the therapist explained that future life progression happens under the state of hypnosis. That is, a pleasant state of relaxation, where the conscious mind can relax and the unconscious mind, which holds a lot of information about our circumstances and emotions, can take over. Her explanation was logical and reassuring - I would always be in control and still able to communicate under hypnosis.

When I came out of my trance, I was flabbergasted. I absolutely couldn't believe that had all been inside my head, and that all it had taken was relaxing and asking the right questions to get it out. It fascinated me that the answers had been inside me all along, blocked only by a lack of knowledge on how to access them.

I began a journey of going within to find the answers to issues I was finding difficult to deal with. This journey would help me connect to the injured parts of myself to find out what they needed so that they could be reassured that they are safe now. It would help me connect to my higher self to keep in touch with what I needed to move through my journey of healing. I did a lot of this through reading, research, journaling, and self-hypnosis. I read many excellent books which have all left a mark, and learned that so many of the answers to my questions lie inside me and can be easily extracted through journaling or self-hypnosis. I did a lot of this also in conjunction with therapists who mentored me and showed me the parts of the puzzle I couldn't see for myself. I value my time with therapists much as someone who wants to get fit values the input of a personal trainer. The ones I felt a rapport with were those who pushed me hard but knew when to tell me I needed to relax and sit in acceptance. I had a laugh with them and cried with them, and learned things on many different layers.

In that first session, I also learned about Ho'oponopono, a Hawaiian spiritual practice for peace. The understanding is that the outside world is a reflection of what is going on inside you, and so if anything is going on that is making you uncomfortable, you can tap into the feeling it is evoking and say,

'I am sorry
Please forgive me
Thank you
I love you'

The belief is that underneath all of our fears, envies, anger and ego we are pure love, and we are apologising for inviting any feelings other than love into our lives.

Hawaiian elders would get tribe members who were arguing together and take them through this process. Many have used it - even as their only spiritual practice - and have witnessed great miracles in their life. I still remember the first time I used it. I was sitting on the sofa at home, my husband and I had just had an argument, and he was now in the kitchen. I felt rubbish. I remembered my therapist's words, shrugged my shoulders, and thought 'it's worth a try!'. I closed my eyes, focused on what had just happened, and said in my head 'I am sorry. Please forgive me. Thank you. I love you.' Within a few moments, my husband came running into the room. 'Are you healing me or something?! I just felt these waves of energy wafting over me.'

I had zero emotional intelligence. My 5-year-old nephew once said to me, 'sometimes I am sad, but I pretend I am angry instead because that's a lot easier.' Well - a 5-year-old had more emotional intelligence than I did because it had taken me until I was in my 30s to realise that I did that too. I was learning from scratch, and what a revelation it was. Learning about the fight and flight response helped me understand what was happening in my body. Learning words for different emotions, by looking at an emotions wheel, helped me express emotions other than 'uncontrollable rage' or 'paralysing anxiety' or 'exhausted depression' - which tends to be where my emotions end up if I don't do anything about them earlier. Learning what to do about emotions before I got to breaking point gave me more energy, more direction, and more space for myself and others in a relationship.

Marriage, and trying to adjust to being a functional human being in one, has taught me to explore what emotions are and how to respond to them rather than be taken over by them. I've learned that it's okay to have needs, and how to state them; how to listen; how to communicate in different styles; how to forgive; how to accept; how to trust the path; how to trust the universe.

It doesn't matter why I didn't have any of these skills. It has certainly been helpful to go back and take a look at past experiences where I responded in ways that were appropriate at the time but no longer serve me. This has helped me understand certain responses and thought patterns I have, and reinforce that things have changed and that I no longer need them. But it's not helpful to dwell. Those lessons were there for a reason - karma, learning - or just to experience. Instead, I focus on what I need to do to move forward and where I want to go, knowing that whilst philosophising on the 'why' is interesting, my experience of feeling freer, lighter, happier, grounded, and steadier as I change my inner conversations is far more relevant to me.

We hold emotions in our bodies. Twice, I have experienced a hypnotherapy session - that is, remember, a conversation had in a relaxed state - completely curing excruciating period pain that I had felt every month for months (the first was just after pregnancy, the second just after surgery). A conversation cured something that painkillers were not touching, something that had had me bed-ridden for days each month. Even as a hypnotherapist, I am still fascinated by its power. I simply talked to my uterus about what it was feeling. It got to express the emotional pain it was feeling, which was a release in itself. I was able to reassure it and reframe the experiences it had had, further reinforcing the healing.

I was so scared by certain things that I was sometimes paralyzed by the fear. I would have panic attacks that left me feeling tense, nauseous, and exhausted for days. Over the years I learned that these were ruled by deeply embedded fears that were unfounded in my current reality. The scared parts of ourselves are there to protect us, and they do a very good job of it. I had to get the part of me that was scared to hop on board to this new paradigm. I had to speak to her, reassure her, understand what she needed, and reframe what had happened to her in light of an adult perspective and new circumstances. I had to keep reminding myself that I am safe, remind myself to breathe, and tell myself to ride the storm until I felt well enough to speak or journal about what was going on. That way I could try and resolve it so that I didn't react the same way again.

There were times that conventional self-care methods such as exercise, journaling, meditation, or talking were not helping - I just couldn't get past the feeling. Time and patience, or a therapy session, helped. On one such occasion I took myself off to the cinema, and for 3 hours I told my mind - 'you sit there and ruminate if you like, or watch the movie. I don't care. I am going to sit here and breathe'. That was a breakthrough moment - a moment in which I realised that I knew my mind was hijacking me, but that I was not my mind - not just because I read it in a book, but because here I was, talking to it as a separate entity. I came out feeling well enough to know I had catastrophized, and well enough to journal about it and come up with a resolution.

A lot of these triggers which had me paralyzed no longer have a hold on me, and I have strong tools to help me through the rest.

Every time I do a journey into healing another part of myself, I feel like the universe conspires to help me. I hear songs to reinforce the lessons. I see signs around me to remind me of the support the universe is providing. I listen to a talk that answers just the question I had on my lips. I get situations, (not always welcome at the time,) where I get to practice the new thought habit - the new response to a trigger. Of course, these "signs" had been there the whole time. There is so much happening around us at any one time that we can't possibly absorb it all and still carry on with our day-to-day existence. So, we filter through these billions of pieces of information and take note of a few. I have merely had my attention drawn to the ones that I am now focusing on instead of the information I was previously focusing on.

In the process of my healing, I discovered lots of methods, and took courses in the ones that resonated with me the most, (hypnotherapy, NLP, and play therapy) to help others. What I love about these techniques is their penchant for tapping into the unconscious mind, and therefore for getting long-term gains from short-term hard work. It's hard work to 'go there'. I have to be like a computer programmer looking for a bug in the code, a mix of study and intuition guiding me to the error. I have to be willing to face my current deepest, darkest, fear. But once 'there' and once the unconscious mind has been brought onside with the conscious mind, my inner conversations are automatically upgraded. I don't have to try and manually insert upgraded beliefs about myself and the safety of the world into my thoughts through affirmations or willpower - which I consider the 'hard way', because they require a constant stream of energy. It is like someone switched on the light and showed me that the 'monster' in the corner was actually a coat, haphazardly thrown onto a chair all along. My life is so different to how it was 6 years ago, and had I not gone on this journey I am pretty sure I would have been in a dark place by now.

Now I realise it's a lifelong quest to return to love. Until I see all as equal, stop taking things personally, accept that all emotions are needed and how to effectively wield their energy, fully trust I will be looked after, and am being looked after no matter what my circumstances are, and accept all parts of myself, I won't be 'there' and in my highest possible reality. And that's okay, because I am loving the journey.

I would like to thank all those who started me on my path - in one sense everyone I have ever met - but key players - Lorraine Flaherty, Marrianne Williamson, Srila Prabhupada, my friends and of course my husband Shyam have been catalysts for my journey.

I am now a clinical hypnotherapist, providing courses on stress and anxiety management. I work with groups and also work with individuals on their awakening journey.

You can find out more about my work here:

www.innerconversations.org

Breaking the spell

Tessa I Richter

Feeling the void,
I've lost all hope.
Where have you gone
My inner song?

Breaking the spell,
hearing your call,
I'm born to life,
ecstatic when done.

Remembered bliss
is faint and far
Visions and dreams
are what is left.

No light to see
Your touch so near
Come take my hand,
Inspire me!

No greater risk
Can I ever take
Than to create
And reconnect..

Risking it all,
I lose control.
Hearing your call
I break the spell...

Tessa I Richter
www.oursecretpotential.com

Words of Wisdom
Audrey Scully

What is Fear?

"Fear is a reaction
Courage is a decision"
-Winston Churchill

We all know the word fear but what does it mean to you? The dictionary definition is 'an unpleasant emotion caused by the threat of danger, pain or harm.'

How often have we experienced fear when there hasn't been any danger, pain or harm present? Many people fear getting up to do public speaking – no threat of danger, harm or pain. However, they may have physical reactions – go white, have tremors etc.

On pondering what I have been fearful of I don't think there is much, if any. Even when I have been in fearful positions, I haven't felt the fear. It has only been recently that I have pondered about this.

The famous quote 'face the fear and do it anyway' reminds me of the times when I was younger and would not say what I wanted to because I thought the outcome would be different – till I did it and it was completely different, in a positive way. Was this a fear or apprehension? No danger, no pain.

There is a huge range of fear – from speaking your truth, to danger – physical, emotional, mental, spiritual. My fear is different to your fear. Your fear is different to my fear.

In my work I learnt that fear is governed by an organ in the body – the kidneys. These get affected when you have any kind of fear. The severity depends on how long you are fearful.

Then again, your fear may be someone else's fear. I am not scared of heights; however, I remember a time when a few of us were walking up an external iron staircase and someone in front of me was terrified. It made me a little scared.

Fear was spread through the media with Covid – this was major fear that spread through the world. Affecting people in different ways. Some were and still are, very fearful.

What is fear? Lack of love, a trigger to help us change what we are fearful of? Disconnection from who we are really are?

So, life is a journey. What if fear is really a gift for us to face it and do it anyway?

Laughter is a healing tool

"I have the power to heal myself,
You have the power to heal yourself,
Together we have the power to heal the world!"
- Dr and Master Zhi Gang Sha

Healing has been a major part of my life and is a major part of everyone's life. We all do it in one form or another. A smile is healing, laughter is healing. It increases our endorphins and dopamine levels; these are our hormones that help us feel happier.

Looking at pictures of me as a child I seemed quite miserable. This wasn't helped by cameras of the time not being able to produce a good picture if people were smiling, I think. Plus, apparently, I could turn on the taps and cry very easily. However, when I reached puberty, I suddenly found things very funny, that actually weren't funny. The time my brother was sat on top of me when we were fighting. I suddenly burst out laughing because I thought the situation was very funny?! He immediately jumped off me and called me mad! WOW! What power, it stopped him fighting me! This realisation only recently came into my awareness. A positive reaction gave me a positive outcome.

Staying on the theme of laughter, this is a huge healing tool. A journalist named Norman Cousins said he had cured himself of a spinal condition with laughter and vitamins!

So, laughter really is the best medicine!

I wonder when the first healing happened, how it happened and if it was realised when it happened?

For me, my path into healing and becoming a Complementary Therapist happened – I used to say 'accidentally', however I now know that nothing happens 'accidentally' or is a coincidence. I love what Abraham Hicks says - 'A coincidence is a co-operative incidence!' It has been pre-planned.

A one-day Reflexology workshop led to a Reflexology qualification. A massage course just to learn how to massage properly turned me into a masseur. A work colleague suggesting I learn Reiki led me to becoming a Reiki Master. An online event led me to become a Tao Hands Practitioner which has rocketed my healing and spiritual expansion.

What I have discovered over the years, and in particular the last year, is that we all have the power to heal ourselves and this has really spurred me on my healing journey to empower people to self-heal.

Love, Expansion & Soul Mission

"Love takes you where you want to be."
- Audrey Scully

Love is a never-ending wheel
Love never ends
Love has many forms
Love is eternal.
There is no lack of love,
Just our mind separating and detaching
From the abundance of love.
The many forms of love –
Maternal, paternal love, sibling love
Love from friendships, romantic relationships
Animals, mother earth, soul, spiritual.
All spiralling, all leading to true love
Unconditional oneness,
Love.

Love is everywhere, even if you are in the depths of despair, love encompasses you. It has many, many forms, from superficial to unconditional. We have experienced many of these forms, searched for love from different people, animals or nature. Looking for someone to give us the love we deserve.

When I left my ex-husband, at times I didn't want to go home – mainly when my son was at his dad's and my house was empty. Then I discovered meditation. I couldn't wait to go home to meditate for 30 minutes. Doing this helped me find inner peace and eventually more self-love. I realised that the love we crave from others is within us. Has always been within us. We just have to find it, connect with it and expand it so we can share it with others and enjoy it.

My cat, (I never thought I would have a pet!), came to me through me attending an Animal Thoughts workshop at the RSPCA in Sheffield. I only went to improve my telepathic skills and help my son's dog and friend's cat. She was 14 and had been with them for a year! Normally 14-year-old cats get adopted very quickly, but she had a few health conditions. I fell in love with her when I went to see her, after she came in our workshop and I stroked her. There is quite a story to this which I may write about one day. The love she gave me was like no other love I had experienced before. It definitely was unconditional and it opened my heart even more. She stayed with me for 2 and a half years and was definitely a soul mate. I am so grateful for her and everything she brought with her.

So, our hearts can be opened in so many different ways. I see so many people drinking when they get hurt. I see so many people go from one relationship to another because they can't be alone. Many of these relationships do not last. If only I could go up to them and ask them to try meditation. It really helped me and still helps me open my heart, go within and find more stillness. It calms me, and gives me the insights and wisdom that expand my awareness, knowledge and love even more.

Pondering on my expansion - I love learning. When I was a Union Steward at the Blood Transfusion Clinic, I went on as many courses as possible. They expanded my knowledge and awareness of how the Union works, how politics work and how we can help staff at our workplace on many levels. I went on confidence, health and safety, equality, media, publicity courses and many more.

This was happening alongside my spiritual awakening and expansion.

The 'AHA' point for me was having this thought whilst I was at my Catholic church, over 24 years ago. 'There has got to be more to life than coming here every week, singing the same hymns, seeing the same people.' Wow! Where did that come from? I actually enjoyed going to church – it helped me through some challenging times and there were a lot of happy times there. I loved being in the choir too.

Soon, a whole new world opened up for me – I discovered that there was more to life, a LOT more. A dear friend passed over and her husband connected me with a 'Medium' whom she had been visiting. From her healing, I went on to visit a Psychic Research Centre with my friend's husband. Little did I know this would be a stepping stone to where I am spiritually today.

We are all spiritual, all on our own level of spirituality, many do not realise this, however many are awakening to this and many are on the escalator, the train, the rocket ship to more spiritual expansion.

Have you ever been surprised how things suddenly fall into place? How something you want or looked for comes to you? Sometimes almost immediately! How you think of someone and they ring you, or you see them? How, when you find yourself looking at your last £10, money comes to you unexpectedly? Or you get the job you wanted, a better house, the friend who fell out with you rings you and apologises?

Why? That is the big question. For me I have learnt that this journey leads us to discover who we truly are. To connect us more to our soul. The disconnection many of us have from birth. My journey is like a big jigsaw coming into the right place at the right time. Each piece connecting with the ones around it. When it does it is AMAZING, magical, even at times unbelievable.

Each piece slowly showing the bigger picture, the picture beyond the human realm, beyond the illusion. A picture with infinite possibilities, infinite opportunities, infinite joy, infinite love, infinite expansion!

To be consciously aware is so empowering. You are much more than your physical self. How exciting is it to know that? Realising that you can go beyond the constraints of human thinking, beyond the ego. You can expand energetically, telepathically, spiritually. You can dive into the inner world, go deeper into that inner world which then manifests the outer world. The inner world which is peace, which is love, which is stillness, which is connection to your soul, which is connection to what some call Source. The more you connect with your inner world the more your outer world changes.

That is what I have discovered since those thoughts in church changed my life. Since my perspective of life changed, and is still continually changing. As this changes, the challenges in my life change -and as I learn the lesson from each one, I find I am less affected, emotionally, mentally, physically and spiritually by it.

Which leads me on to soul mission. We all want to know what our soul mission is. Many search for it, for many years. I have learned what it is and it is very simple. As I write this the thought has come to me – soul mission is not purpose in life.

My present understanding is there are many purposes in our lives – being a parent, being a student, the job you are in, the social life you have. For me, I think my main purpose is to never stop learning, gain wisdom so I can help others more, open my heart, love more, serve others more.

Within the last year I have learnt that my soul mission is to serve my soul, so it too can expand and grow through my experiences. And to continually work on myself to be more loving, kind, forgiving, compassionate, grateful, harmonious, abundant, humble, enlightened and to serve humanity.

My journey from awareness to the present day, being on a spiritual rocket ship has been one of unfurling and understanding how life can become more amazing every day.

Learning how to release and let go of hurts and disappointments.
How to go to the depths and rise up again stronger and wiser.
How we have separated ourselves from each other and from our souls.
How can we reconnect to all of those?
How important forgiveness and gratitude are for our spiritual journey.
They are food for the soul.
Forgiveness brings inner peace and joy.
Gratitude is the key to progress; it also brings a deeper sense of peace.
Expressing gratitude and feeling gratitude aligns you more to your true nature. You are stepping more in the flow of the universe.
Most importantly, we are all connected.
We are all one.
When we live in the Oneness our blockages disappear
And we become one with Source.

Dedicated to my brother, Steven Scully and also Pat and Kenny Barker.

Audrey is a transformational Healer, Mentor and Speaker. She works with both body and energy and uses many modalities including Chi-Reflexology, Reconnective Healing, Tao Hands Healing, Reiki and Seichem. She empowers women to reconnect with their self-worth and build confidence in all aspects of their life.

As well as being a bespoke funeral celebrant, she is also a mother, Grandmother and soon-to-be Great-Grandmother, who loves the JOYful things in life!

You can connect with her here:
www.audreyscully.com
FB: Audrey Scully – PURITY Natural Healing
*Twitter: @PURITYhealing_*

The Bystander

Shelina Jaffer

I look at myself in a mirror
And see a tall figure Gazing back at me
Long dark hair, deep brown eyes
Gazing back, In search of answers

Who am I, I ask myself ?
Am I a mother, a wife or a daughter?
Am I a sister, a friend or a partner?
Am I a Teacher or a Student?
A Doctor or a Patient?

I know I am not what I wear, as these change every day
And I am not what I say, as this changes in what, when and where
I am not a name on the door or the markings on the floor.

What I do know is that I am a living, breathing being
Sitting, standing, walking, talking
A being with feelings and emotions
Memories and thoughts

I sit back and look at my past, my present and my future
My dreams and aspirations, my achievements and goals
And yet I am not these sentiments
I am just the bystander, watching as these thoughts go by

I am this bystander, looking back at myself
Looking at my thoughts, my life, my experiences
Watching the world as it goes by
Watching as it all changes, whilst I remain the same

This bystander that is calm and clear
Clear and certain
Certain and strong
This bystander that watches and learns
Knows and Trusts
This bystander that sometimes gets lost
Lost in the excitement and the chaos of the world
Lost in the mayhem of thoughts
Thoughts that taint that certainty and knowing
Lost in the grey clouds of feelings
Feelings that harbour self-doubt and fear

And all along
Gazing onwards
I know that it will all work out
I know that this chaos will fade.

But to STOP for a moment
And let the thoughts settle
Let the fear subside

Just a breath of air
One then another, and another
In and Out

And as the clouds break, the rays of Hope shine through
Certainty and confidence emerge
And creativity flows

And I now know that it's not the clothes that I wear
Or the words that I say.
I am that mother, wife and daughter
I am that sister, friend and partner

And I am that bystander-
Calm and clear
Clear and certain
Certain and strong.
This bystander that watches and learns
Knows and Trusts
That is who I am.

Shelina Jaffer

My Awakening
Becky Stanton

Awakening. What is an awakening?

If you'd asked me 10 years ago, the word wouldn't have made sense to me. "I am awake. If I pinch myself, I can feel it. I'm here, aren't I?"

If you'd asked me 7 years ago, I was coming to the realisation that perhaps I had been asleep. Stuck in unhelpful patterns. Going around in circles. Following the pack instead of my intuition. Walking around in a zombie haze in my 9-5. And realising that maybe I was the problem. Perhaps I was the reason I'd been so unhappy.

If you'd asked me 3 years ago, I *felt* awakened. I had quit my career, started a business as a Mindset Coach, and felt aligned with my passions. I had discovered manifestation and was seeing how powerful I was in this world. I felt happy. I felt grounded. I felt divinely connected with everything.

And if you ask me today, I feel awakened and more one with this Universe than ever before.. Yet I would tell you ***I'm still waking up.***

Why?

Because I've come to realise that life is an awakening.

... And the reason we've been put on this Earth is to wake up. Beautiful souls in human bodies, with a soul contract to awaken.

That's the purpose. To expand into our truest, soulful, limitless selves. Through lifetimes. Through cycles. Through adversity.

There's no rush. There's no deadline. There's no urgency to have it all figured out and be "awakened".

It's a beautiful, divine journey with no definitive 'end' destination. We live in a limitless Universe. There is more and more and more to learn, experience, and awaken to.

We're continuously waking up to higher perspectives, higher timelines, higher frequencies. Seeing our world through higher dimensional lenses.

So how do we awaken?

The good news is awakening is the most natural thing for us to do. And we do it through living life!

When we participate in this world, we naturally awaken.

In fact, we're *designed* to awaken. Through interactions with others, through relationships, through pursuing our dreams, through trying and failing and growing, and through unexpected challenges.

When you're aware of it and you start living consciously, you see that every single moment is an awakening. An invite into a higher perspective. An invite to dive deeper into yourself.

But there are certain phases of life that are deeply intense as you awaken to new levels and re-calibrate your whole being more quickly.

It's why you see the memes of awakenings looking like torture!

You expect the awakening to be another, beautiful, unfolding eye-opening experience, when really, it's an intense death and a rebirth.

Death of the ego and old identity
Rebirth of who you really are

You're saying goodbye to the version of you that you know well and feel attached to.
And tentatively saying hello to a new version of you that you've never experienced before.

It feels uncertain
It feels scary
It feels painful

A part of you is dying... So that you can transcend.

But it's messy.
It's confusing.
You're questioning everything.
You're seeing things differently.
Physically, you can actually see things differently.

In my current awakening, I'm seeing the world energetically - like the matrix. I see energy. I see beyond the matter. I know it's temporary as I adjust. But this is how it's affecting me physically.

And during this time, the human ego has a field day.

But here's the thing, the ego isn't bad. It just prefers stability, safety and protection. It's your hyper-sensitive and boisterous security guard. It's holding you back for security purposes. This awakening is its worst nightmare - so it goes into hyper-safety mode.

And whilst the ego has good intentions, it can feel like a leech sucking the last ounce of energy you have.

I've experienced both awakenings on my soul path.

The unfolding *and* the rebirth.
Both equally as beautiful.

What has been really powerful for my awakening journey is choosing to see life as an awakening. Choosing to expect quantum growth all the time. Choosing to allow the complex emotions to be met. Choosing to befriend the ego. Choosing to awaken with the divine love that surrounds me.

It's a choice.
A choice you can make right now.
A choice you learn from and grow into!

Awakening Lessons

I am a super reflective Pisces that loves to analyse my soul path journey. Every step has been meaningful and expansive (even if I didn't see it or appreciate it at the time).

I can see 5 phases that I've been through already in my 35 years here on Earth. The past 4 phases alone have been in the last 7 years. And I'm going through a deep death and rebirth right now as I write this. *Divine timing.*

Phase 1: Powerless

My story is one of feeling not enough and not worthy. So much so that I mentally took myself out of the game. I was still playing the game of life - school, University, corporate ladder - but sheepishly following the flock. Truthfully, I felt like a nobody flowing through life. Waiting for life to happen to me.

I felt powerless. I felt unworthy. I felt lost. I felt unfulfilled. I felt unhappy.

Phase 2: My Saturn Return - a death + rebirth

By my mid-20's, I was nearing burnout already. I was working in Human Resources in luxury retail, pulling fourteen-hour days in the office. It was chaotic and *I* was chaotic. The only way I knew how to control the chaos was to work harder and work longer. A pattern I'd seen in my parents.

Fortunately, an angel (disguised as my manager and now very close friend), forced me to take a three-week holiday.

I took myself to Italy for a solo trip. To breathe. To flow. To be.

I went from 14 hour jam-packed days full of HR drama and disputes to calmly meandering Italian streets with a gelato in the September sunshine. And the best part? There was zero agenda.

Without the noise of daily life, I was starting to see and feel magic every single day.

I was waking up to a world outside of my beige hamster wheel. And it was eye opening.

When I headed back to London, I felt refreshed and happy. I'd had time to reflect on what I wanted and I knew it wasn't this job or this fast-paced lifestyle.

I looked for a new job and found one in luxury fashion. But instantly I knew the job was wrong. I still felt so unhappy. Unsatisfied. Unfulfilled.

I knew I needed to leave. Leave my HR career. Leave this path I was on. I didn't like where it was headed. It felt like I would be coasting through life forever if I stayed where I was.. And that wasn't what I wanted for myself anymore. I wanted *more.*

My soul was calling out for change.

But I'd never connected to this part of me before. I didn't understand it. And I didn't give myself much space to listen.

It would come through loudly in moments of silence. I'd hear it, feel it, sense it. "There's more than this. I'm meant for more."

But I was closing this voice down throughout the day. Like an ostrich with its head blissfully in the sand.

Yet, that soulful voice remained. And when you ignore soul guidance, it gets louder and more obvious until it's heard.

...That's exactly what happened next.

With the support of a Counsellor and Life Coach - both entered my life unexpectedly and free (thank you Universe) - magic started unfolding as I reconnected with myself, my passions, and my desired life.

I quit my job with a vision of being my own boss, doing something I loved. I didn't know what that was yet, but a part of me knew it would become clear.

I felt awake. I felt in control. I felt powerful.

But then fear creeped in through the rear door, pushed my soul to the passenger seat and took control of the steering wheel.

Fear was leading me.

"Who am I to do this? Who am I really? What if it doesn't work out? What will people think? What will people say? What if I let people down? What if I embarrass myself? What if I never make money? What if I fail? What if I succeed and can't handle it?"

I was in my head. Over and over and over. The same fears. The same worries. The same doubts.

The 3 months were getting closer and closer. I had no plan, no ideas, no motivation.

I was given an opportunity to extend my notice. I ended up working 9 months - clinging on to this old identity for dear life.

I chose the soul nudge. Yet the fear was fighting to keep me safe. Keep me with what felt familiar. Keep me from failing.

This is what led me down the beautiful path of mind-set work. I started to heal my limiting beliefs that were creating the fear. And I knew that I was destined to support women in the same way.

I retrained as an NLP Mindset Coach. I reconnected with my power. I saw time and time again how my thoughts became things in my reality.

This awakening was waking me up to the power of my thoughts, beliefs and choices. I saw that I had more power than ever before. And that it was safe to trust myself. To trust the soulful nudges. To trust something beyond me.

My soul path led me to manifestation. And I was manifesting the most incredible things quickly - soul clients, money, experiences, connections.

Phase 3: An Energetic World

Business and life felt so aligned and so beautiful. I was happy, I was grateful, I was grounded, and I was a master manifester.

My mind had freed me from playing the victim. Yet, I felt like I'd hit a ceiling. I felt limited. I felt closed in.

I had seen first-hand with myself and clients how powerful mindset and manifestation rituals were, and I was being guided to awaken into new energetic levels.

I was ready to expand into higher perspectives! I had a sense that my mind could only take me so far.

I was ready to expand beyond the mind. Into a world that was energetically connected to everything and everyone.

This awakening was a gradual unfolding. Day by day I was being invited to see the world through an energetic lens.

The more I cleansed and expanded my energy, the more magic I would experience. I was being introduced to new energetic principles, healers, groups, classes, books.

I retrained with energy - diving deep with reiki, chakras, and activations.

My life expanded beautifully. I could protect my energy, call it back, cleanse it, and expand it.

And I was seeing the results expand for my clients too. When we freed the limitations from their mind as well as their body and energy - there was no stopping them! They were free.

Now I know this awakening phase was preparing me to dive even deeper spiritually. Preparing me for what was to come.

Phase 4: Divine order and Divine abundance

I had great experience with the "I want it, I got it" manifestation energy. Ariana's song was my theme tune.

I tuned into my desires, energetically aligned and embodied the desire, and it would manifest in my reality most of the time. I would teach and coach my clients this process too and they would manifest the most incredible experiences.

Yet, often, the manifestations wouldn't last. Quantum leaps would leap in all directions after a while.

It felt like a struggle or an uphill effort to be consistent.

And then it dawned on me... What if they are ego manifestations? What if the desires are surface level and that's why they don't stick around? That maybe they're not truly soul aligned and destined on our soul path. They are forced. They are manipulated energy.

This awakening phase was truly letting go and surrendering to the divine order and divine abundance of the Universe.

I needed to go through that experience to reconnect with my true essence and my power. I knew how connected, one, and magical the Universe is now.

I get to let go.

Let go of control
Let go of coercion
Let go of deadlines
Let go of forcing
Let go of material wins

This has been a powerful awakening phase reconnecting me with my soul path. Reconnecting me with my purpose, my mission, my passions.

I still have a vision, tune into my desires and set intentions. Yet now, I trust that everything is unfolding perfectly for my highest good and everyone's highest good. Naturally.

It's no longer all on my shoulders.

I am a powerful co-creator.

I tune into my soulful self, I follow the breadcrumbs, I enjoy the journey.

Knowing everything is working out. It's a powerful awakening to my soul path for a much more enjoyable life experience as I grow and expand!

Phase 5: [untitled] - a death + rebirth

This is the phase I'm currently in - and it's a rebirth. An intense, world-shaking, powerful rebirth.

In the space of 3 months, I experienced great loss. I miscarried a baby and my dad passed away unexpectedly shortly after.

This was the first time in my life that I had ever faced loss like this before. In a way, I had feared it happening to me for years.

Yet it was strangely beautiful.

I know and trust that the first 4 phases of my awakening were preparing me for this phase.

To mourn the loss on a human level. To truly honour my emotions. To give myself the space I needed. To care for my physical body. To be kind and gentle with my thoughts. To protect my energy from others. To be present in this moment.

And yet, on a spiritual level, feel so deeply connected with both the spirit of my baby and my dad.

It was a human, 3D, physical loss.
It was not a spiritual loss. It was a deepening. *It was an awakening.*

To how connected and one we really are.

And this is the phase I'm still in.

I still cry randomly. I still get triggered. I'm still healing.

Yet, something magical is unfolding. I feel more connected than I ever have before. I know I am spiritually loved and guided by these souls. They are in my spirit team with me every step.

And I have a new, beautiful perspective on life... and death.

I see my dad for who he truly is. I honour his flaws. They were human flaws. And I see and appreciate his soul that lives on.

The best part of him lives on with me. And guides me every day.

I've seen that the worst possible thing that I feared, has actually been the most powerful, transformational experience of my entire life.

I'm awakening to new levels of consciousness.

Grasshopper Guidance:

One hot summer's day, while writing this chapter, I was in my garden tuning into my awakening journey.

Moments before, I had seen a grasshopper in a spider's web and decided to free it. Usually I don't interfere with nature, but my intuition said to do it.

As I was laying in the grass, who joins me to sunbathe? The grasshopper.

As I watched this beautiful creature hop around across blades of grass, I instantly knew this was a message for me. A message to share with you in my chapter.

The message is this: ***have faith and the courage to hop.***

Awakening is a series of hops - some small, some gigantic. The key is to trust and let go.

Trust your soul path
Let everything else go

If you truly believe you're here to awaken to higher possibilities and higher dimensions, you will. Your focus and responsibility is to prioritise tuning into your soulful self, act on the intuitive guidance you're being shown, stay committed to your vision and...

Trust and let it go.

Stay in your soul path lane, beautiful soul. It's easy to get brushed along with other people's journeys and start comparing and measuring your life success.

Trust and let it go.

It's also easy to get caught up in your head - your thoughts, your beliefs, your worries, your anxieties, your fears. It's human. See it as a challenge to expand yourself.

Trust and let it go.

It's human to focus on the outcome and try to make it happen. There's deep conditioning before your higher awakening that that's how the world works. You're in control.

Trust and let it go.

There will be moments where you don't want to awaken anymore. You'll just want to feel safe and secure and stay still for one. That's okay. Do what you need to and...

Trust and let it go.

So what is awakening to me now?

It's acceptance
It's waking up to see beyond 3D reality
It's waking up to see higher possibilities

It's realising how magical this world is
It's seeing the connection, oneness and miracles that is life
It's slowing down to witness them

It's letting go of how you are conditioned to see the world
It's seeing the world through a clearer lens
It's witnessing the magic before your eyes
It's trusting the magic that you cannot see

It's feeling all the feels
It's making peace with fear and ego
It's making peace with your past
It's making peace with your future
It's releasing the conditioning

It's handing over the details
It's letting go of micro-managing and manipulating life
It's loosening your grip on life
It's surrendering to the divine flow of life
It's trusting that everything always works in your highest favour
It's expecting magic

It's realising that you are the Universe
It's realising that you are magic
It's realising that anything in this magical Universe is a reflection of you
It's realising you can receive anything you desire

It's waking up to the divine flow of life
And playing in this game of life!
Because it's all to play for - and you're the winning piece.

I'm so grateful to awaken with you, beautiful soul xxx

Becky Stanton is a Soul-led Mindset + Manifestation Coach for female entrepreneurs.

Her mission is to empower women to believe in themselves, know their worth, and stand in their power so they confidently follow their wildest passions + desires to live happy, fulfilled lives!

Becky passionately believes there is not one way to create success and encourages you to throw out the rulebook! She's here to guide you back to reclaiming your POWER, knowing that any limitations have been learnt + can be released. So you can believe + trust more deeply in yourself and this beautiful magnetic Universe we live in.

Her signature offers guide entrepreneurial women to grow their businesses with an abundant, miracle mindset and in full alignment with their soul's path. As when you're in alignment with your truest self, you'll be a magnet to all that you desire!

Website:

www.beckystanton.com

Social Media:

Instagram:
https://www.instagram.com/beckystanton_mindset coach/

Facebook:

https://www.facebook.com/beckystantonmindsetcoach/

Pinterest:
https://tr.pinterest.com/beckystanton_mindsetcoach/

Intuition
Siobhan Louise

Intuition is the anchor that I cast into the deep knowing of the universe.
The connection between me and the vastness.
Tethering me to truth.
Guiding me home like stars in the night.
A compass that encompasses me.

Intuition is the sound of resonance.
Of the harmonics of the ether, reverberating within.
It's the frequency of my soul's knowing and the trust in my reception of melody.
The ever-unfolding aria and the unison of my earthly voice.

Intuition is trusting, in the subtleties we sense.
The smell of rain. The stench of fear.
The flash of danger before it plays out.
The feeling in the pit of my stomach, telling me someone or a situation is draining my energy.
The high alert.

Intuition is the flow, the pull.
The hunger of need and the thirst of desire.
The magnetism to those who hold lessons and blessings.
A euphoric high that draws you to riches your soul longs for.
The map of your life in invisible ink.

Intuition is the cosmic unfolding.
A crystalline reflection.
The guiding force of nature.
The dé·jà vu of life.

From Songs of the Soul by Siobhan Louise.

A Letter
Elisha Ward

What is crying out to be said?

The world is hungry for it.

Yet too many are beating around the bush
Fearful of stepping out of line, out of place
Of really being seen for their incredible selves

Thinking of blending in, yet needing to stand out

Doing what they feel they must,
Just to get through the day
To earn that money, to feel validated

And there's an issue, a real problem there
An ache
A gaping wound that is being ignored
And can never be solved or healed that way

We need to take a look at it
See it
Squarely in the face
Love it
Bring just buckets and buckets of love
And feel that just heal right up

Coming strongly, powerfully,
Standing up as you
Standing in your truth as love and spirit
All that ever was and all that ever will be

You have it
You are it
There's nothing but you

What could possibly be lacking?

Look at your beauty
Your tremendous beauty and strength
Your power takes my breath away

I adore what you do
How you move
What comes through you
When you allow yourself to be fully guided
And to love fiercely
Wholeheartedly

Is there fear?
Perhaps so, but it is no issue
It's no impediment
There is only love
Shine that love

Let us feel you
Let us see you
See your magnificence

Please bestow your brilliance on us
Move mountains

Let us feel your heart
Experience your knowing
And your incredible beauty

You are here
I am here
This is a marvellous adventure
Filled with exquisite wonder
Why don't you jump right in?

Gorgeous one,
You are needed
I mean YOU are needed
Not the shell, the mask you put forwards
But YOU in your full opulence

You in full flow
In your element
No holds barred
Creative and shining and beautiful

Giving all of you
Everything you have
And getting it all back to you in return too
Being filled up
So full
Overflowing
Bursting with love and light

You are magnificent
I just adore you
Spending time, my life, eternity with you
Is an incredible sweet joy
It is a pleasure like no other

To feel you
To taste your heart

I am in awe of it
You are mighty
Please let us hear you roar

What needs to be said?
What wants to come through you?
Will you allow it?
Will you let us see your beautiful heart?

We love you
I love you
I've always loved you
There is nothing here but you

Let us dance together for all eternity
Back and forth
Round and round
In a continual
Ever evolving
Ever unfolding dream of epic proportions
That was never born and will never die

I am you
And you are me
And the love is out of this world
It's quite literally not of this world

There is such power in deciding you are who you are
And having no fear about that
Because you are what God made you to be
You are his entire intention made manifest in the world

Who are you to reject you?
Can't you see the beauty that shines out of every part of you?
Allow him to work you
Feel the love
That tremendous energy, spirit

That feeling that there's more to come
That is you
That is the truth of you
That box is not you

You are beyond time and space
Your magnificence knows no bounds

The world was created for you to play in
Your playground
The backdrop to the game,
All put there for you to enjoy.
To know yourself in limitless myriad ways
Bring it all close
See the beauty of a flower, of an item of clothing, of your heart
All of it is you.
Aren't you beautiful?
You are here.
It's all here and it's all for you
I love you.

Elisha Ward
www.elishaward.com

Reflections
Debbie Sutherland

Fear

I realise, looking back, I had always lived in close proximity to fear. Not terrifying fear, small fears. Tiny fears really, that accumulate over time. Fears that keep a person small.

Fear mostly occupied my head space. An inner dialogue asking what if? What if I get laughed at? What if it doesn't work out? What if I can't cope? What if someone can do it better? What if I do it wrong?

Who knows where my propensity for fear came from? Certainly not from my peaceful and happy childhood. Maybe it started that first time I was laughed at or belittled at school. Maybe it started after the first small failure that I don't even remember now it was so insignificant. I don't know for sure, but it's there.

Fear muted my colours. It wound its way around my heart and moved me away from love and joy. If I was truly living from love my "what if" questions would be very different. What if it all worked out better than I imagined? What if it all went perfectly? What if I was successful beyond my wildest dreams?

Fear is obviously extremely useful in keeping us safe from direct harm. The crash helmet, the seat belt, the rules that keep us safe. But some of my fears were keeping me safe from imaginary harm. My fears made me create my own rules. I don't do public speaking that was a rule. I don't ask for anything in case I get turned down and humiliated, another rule. I don't take risks.

Using fear as a compass I would avoid the job application for the job that might require public speaking. I wouldn't pursue the relationship in case it ended badly.

So, when I experienced infertility, my fears went into overdrive. I broke my own heart daily with my pervasive and fearful thoughts. What if I never become a mum? What if I can't cope with this grief? What if I let my partner down?

My obsessive thoughts about infertility were keeping me in a constant state of fight or flight. I was on autopilot most of the time. I was always seeking outside help for my "problem". Looking to others to fix it, to fix me. Acupuncturists, reflexologist, counsellors, homeopaths, and psychics. But, transmuting this fear had to become an inside job.

Awareness/transition

I walked into the room on my first day of the mindfulness resilience course and looked around at everyone sat in a circle, all with their own reasons for being there. The teacher sat amongst them, emanating calm. I thought I was there to learn skills to help my sick patients at work. I soon realised this is what I needed.

Within the first hour the mindfulness teacher had cracked open my belief system and I could see a way forward. He explained how our thoughts about a situation are often far worse than the reality. That what we experience may cause us pain, (primary suffering) but the stories we layer over that experience cause additional and optional pain (secondary suffering).

As I mentioned earlier, I was breaking my own heart daily with my internal stories about my infertility. This mindfulness all seemed very plausible, but how did I stop these stories from playing over and over in my head and adding to my suffering? And his answer? - we don't! We don't stop the stories, we just become aware of them. And, in our awareness, they lose their power. In our awareness, we can question their truth. In our awareness, we can imagine a different possibility.

Over the next few weeks and months, I learned to question my thoughts. Apparently, thoughts are not facts! I did not have to believe any of them. I also learned to cope with uncertainty. One of the things I found most difficult to deal with during infertility was the uncertainty. I like an end goal, a plan, and a timeline. That is just my way. Infertility, with absolutely no certainty whatsoever, was sending me spiralling. One of my beautiful mindfulness teachers helped me to reframe uncertainty. He said that the greatest thing about uncertainty is that anything can happen. So, for every negative outcome I could imagine, there is an equal and opposite amazing potential outcome. I may become a mum of triplets, I may adopt, I may live happily childless, who knew?

Through the mindfulness classes I learned to sit and watch my thoughts. When I was a little girl, my dad used to take me and my sister to a garden centre where they had a display of gnomes. He told us that the gnomes came to life and danced, but only when we weren't looking. We would spend ages pretending not to look, sneaking glances from the corner of our eyes to see if we could catch them dancing. We never did. Fears are just like those gnomes. They will run riot around your mind while you are busy doing other things (subconsciously controlling you) but, as soon as you turn to face them, they stop. They dissolve. They can't stand up to your scrutiny. Just bringing awareness to them weakens their power.

My future was uncertain, but, in those moments of meditation practice in the hot classroom that summer, there was no past, no future. Just me, sat in the chair, breathing in, breathing out. Relief flooded my body.

Healing/Integration

Now I had work to do. I had found mindfulness. Within days it eased my fear. But I wasn't always going to be in the classroom sitting with my teacher. Without a regular practice those fears were going to start running the show again. I had to integrate this practice into my life. It was hard work. After all, I had been this way for almost forty years. Mindfulness doesn't just switch it off. There is no end point to this journey, to this practice of mindfulness.

My regular meditation practice began. I tagged it onto my morning routine. I finished my breakfast and set my timer. I got comfortable and closed my eyes, I fidgeted, I opened one eye, closed it again. I thought a million thoughts, fidgeted some more, thought some more. I forgot I even had breath to watch, fidgeted again and longed for the timer to ping. This was going to be tough!

I wanted to give up before I even got started. I spoke to my meditation Teacher. He smiled his serene smile knowingly. Apparently, this is normal. So, I sat again and again and again, and each time it got a little easier. I was having periods of peace, just watching the breath, no thoughts for short periods, and when thoughts came up, I was aware. The fears came, but sometimes I could catch them before they triggered the fear response in my body. "It's just a thought", I would whisper. The fears couldn't get close enough to carry me off down the rabbit hole. Sometimes these seated practices gave me a safe space to hold a fearful thought up for scrutiny. To examine it from all angles, consciously. To journal afterwards and take control of my response. I was creating space between me and my fears. They weren't crowding me anymore.

Often the way you approach a practice like mindfulness will give you great insight into the way you approach life. I noticed that I was often impatient to get to the end of the practice, frustrated at my lack of focus. Fidgety, agitated and usually afraid that I was missing something somewhere else. Through my new-found awareness, I realised that I was bringing all these qualities to my quest for motherhood. I was impatient, making decisions based on fear because I felt I was losing my opportunity and running out of time. I was flitting from one healing modality to another impatiently.

Love/Expansion/ soul mission

Meditation practice became my port in the storm of infertility. It brought a calm feminine yin quality to the masculine yang approach I had brought thus far to becoming a mum.

Some days my meditation practice would take me in to a deep sense of peace. I was able to lean back into that space of awareness more and more often. Pure awareness is magical. It is just spaciousness. There is no pain, no infertility, only awareness. The part of me that is aware of my thoughts is above all the pain.

My ability to cope grew. My resilience grew. When I was presented with fertility treatment opportunities, I chose the most loving option for me and my family. I didn't choose the option that would get me there fastest. I turned down treatment cycles to allow my body to rest and recover. I learned self-compassion. I had been judging myself and my body harshly for its “failings”. Now I had new compassion practices to soothe myself. I could lay my hand on my heart and feel the warmth soothing my whole body. I could stop the deprecating self-talk in its tracks through my awareness and choose more loving thoughts.

Infertility is a unique kind of grief and brings with it a sense of isolation. One of the elements of mindfulness and self-compassion is common humanity. Recognising that you are not alone in your experience brings great comfort. The idea that this is all part of a shared human experience, and we are all connected brought me comfort in dark times. Knowing that one day I would share this experience with other infertile women gave meaning to my pain.

And now, I am a mother to a beautiful soul! And a whole new set of fears that come with motherhood! My son has been my greatest teacher through his natural presence and ease of being. I would not change one step of this journey so far. I am so grateful for the lessons and the opportunity to alchemise this fear and brokenness into wholeness.

As we move through uncertain times, fear is inevitable. I feel fear often, but it is no longer trapped in my body or my mind. It's not hiding in the shadows subversively controlling me. It's out where can see it. It's front and centre in my awareness, where I can converse with it. I don't have to fear fear. Through awareness and compassion, I transmute it into love.

Debbie lives with her partner and six-year-old son in Sheffield. After 25 years working for the NHS as a nurse, she now loves to combine her knowledge, wisdom, and experience of healing in the western medical system with her passion for complementary health care.

As a Reiki Practitioner, Aromatherapist, doTERRA Wellness Advocate, and Mindfulness Guide she helps women connect to their innate resources to feel calm and resilient through ritual and presence.

Debbie can be found on Instagram and Facebook @ herhealinghub. She shares a wealth of information and her available workshops on her website: www.debbie-sutherland.com

Truth and Beauty
Elaine Trippett

Secrets whispered
Breathy words
Regrets maybe
They must be heard
Dust on the wind
Turning over the cards
I told her softly
I wish I hadn't worked so hard.

He bought me flowers
But only the once
He told me he loved me
But only in his glance
I bottled up emotions
Sometimes quiet was my healing
But mostly I wish
I'd had the courage to express my feelings.

And I sent her letters and
Wrote postcards
Talked on the phone

When times were hard
I still don't know what I did to offend
But I wish I'd the notion
why she stopped being my friend.

I lived through others
I thought it enough
To serve with quiet
To smile with love
But I know there were times
I was almost on pause
Didn't try to be happy
As my own focus cause.

I can only say
What I can see
My own truth is
In the heart of me
Was my life true
The essence of me?
Or did I only reflect
The image others expected of me?

A camellia flower
Or a blade of grass
A perfect snowflake
Or green sea glass

A lover's eyes
Or a hand clasped close
Truth and beauty
Regrets now go.

Elaine Trippett – Singer/Songwriter & Poet
Facebook: The Domino Effect

Being Present in Every Moment

Emma Brown

Hello beautiful souls. I hope that if you are struggling with awakening and the confusing and difficult things it brings up for you, that our words will help you find faith in yourself and your ability to navigate it. Aside from seeking advice and wisdom from others, ultimately, I believe all strength and answers lie within ourselves. We just have to be brave enough to really look and listen deeply, compassionately and unconditionally.

The things that happen to us don't define us. We define ourselves.

One of the main things I have learned is to trust the process. I know this is a cliché saying, but this quote by one of my favourite authors perfectly sums up the depth of meaning behind this statement. "For a seed to achieve its greatest expression, it must come completely undone, the shell cracks, its inside come out and everything changes. For someone who doesn't understand growth, it would look like complete destruction." ~ Cynthia Occelli.

This quote, for me, has been very influential in helping me trust the process, whilst swirling down the rapids of my mental health journey to calmer waters. It applies to almost everything. Small and large scale. Personal growth, life, parenting, relationships, setting up a business, producing a painting, the evolution of humanity, economic and environmental crisis. I believe that to reach a place of true expansion, completeness and balance, we must experience difficult and often painful, confusing things in life. It helps us to really understand the whole. To fully appreciate the joys and wonders of life. It helped me to take deep breaths and simply trust that something amazing was happening, and that deeply spiritual teachings could be attained if I could truly be present with my fear, pain and anger.

My earliest really profound spiritual awakening came when my older brother died in a motorbike accident. I was 24 and 6 months pregnant with my son (2nd child). The thing that struck me most, alongside the grief and shock, was something I still find difficult to put into words. There was an intense, exquisite beauty to it. To the depth of human emotion, the likes of which I had never before experienced or personally witnessed. To the revelation of so many more questions about life and death, and how they are so perfectly intertwined and inseparable.

I sometimes think people consider me crazy when I try to explain this. It just cracked me - and everything I saw, felt and had ever believed in - wide open. Anything insignificant or unimportant seemed to vanish. There was such a sense of clarity. About how precious life is and how we should focus on what's really important. But equally the pain was unfathomable at the time.

However, I quickly buried a lot of my own grief so that I could focus on bringing another human into the world and somehow try to console my parents. After several more traumas and difficult life experiences I reached a point where I could no longer keep all this stuff buried and I had no other choice but to face it. My mental health was suffering greatly because I hadn't processed my own emotions properly. It took me many years to reach this point and to begin healing my wounds with the help of some wonderful therapists and talking to family and friends.

I have learned to be present with others in their pain without trying to fix everything. To just listen - holding space for them to feel safe in expressing whatever they need to express. But, the hardest thing has been to do that for myself. To really love myself in the face of shame, guilt and feelings of ugliness and inadequacy. Yet, the peace of mind and sense of being complete is astronomical when I do achieve it. It gives me so much courage to carry on, to show up and to just be me. To wholeheartedly love and accept myself as I am in any given moment. To show up no matter how I feel, even if showing up means staying in bed and resting but being fully present with my feelings and needs. Exhausted, feeling unloved or unlovable, yet honouring the space and time I need to return to feeling refreshed and worthy.

We need to recognise when our cup is empty and needs filling with the things we know will fill it. Subsequently, we can then help others better too. Some days are still tough. I still get it wrong or forget my boundaries and how to give myself what I need. But finding a quiet moment and putting all my strength into being present always seems to bring me home again.

Like the other day for instance. I was sat in my car in the car park, waiting for my youngest (15 years) to finish her therapy session - feeling like I had given all I had to give. It had been a particularly difficult, draining and demanding week. I stopped. I refrained from putting music on or going on social media. I stared blankly ahead as my mind struggled to be present. I looked. I listened. I felt. I breathed. I tasted. I tried to meditate. A distant drilling noise felt intrusive. I noticed so many things. The sound and feel of energy waves all around me.

My mind swirled and swelled with dozens of thoughts. My head was buzzing like an electric meter. Brain fog started to creep in again. I noticed the tightness in my chest. I noticed the awareness that it was caused by so much more than my most recent bout of Covid. My mind, like a pinball, was flicked again. This time by the media-fuelled fear of the possibility of Britain going to war with Russia.

I tried again to meditate. To find that inner peace. That stillness. Breathing slowly and deeply. The sound of the wind and the rain softly nudging against the car, gave me a gentle jolt and a warm childhood memory. I couldn't quite place the memory but it felt like a holiday memory, maybe in Scotland. It was more of a feeling though. It had one of those madly profound flash effects of remembering who I am. The real and wild me.

Does that happen to you?

I love these moments. Remembering my pure spirit. Joy. Wonder. Love. Before all the self-conscious battles my mind wrapped itself around so very tightly and tied itself up in knots about. Before all our human conditioning and programming. Before the invasion of our sovereignty.

"THAT is who I want to be!" cried my inner child.

That free, pure spirit. Before all the bullying, trauma, abuse, loss, grief, sadness, guilt, fear, heartache, control, self-hate, helplessness, shame, perceived inadequacy... and exhaustion. Before never feeling like enough. That pure spirit that felt like enough.

"How can I get back to her?" my heart sighed.

"I am so much more than enough" I whispered to myself. "I always have been. I always will be. I am her."

I found my way back again.

It's a daily, sometimes hourly, sometimes minute by minute thing. Finding my way back. Back to my spirit. Back to Source. Back to truth. Back to the present moment. Which really is where all the magic seems to live. In fully experiencing what the present moment holds. Whether that is painful or joyful. In being fully conscious and aware of our thoughts and feelings and fully responsible for our words and behaviours.

Taking responsibility for our own actions, words and circumstances can initially be riddled with guilt and shame. But, when we realise that we really have ultimate control over our own lives, the liberation is powerful. If we're careful with our thoughts and language - to ourselves and others- and with our breath work, I believe we can transform anything.

I still sometimes grieve the loss of who I was. The pure me that nothing bad happened to. The woman I could have been if my life had been different. I have to remind myself regularly that I cannot ever be a person all that bad stuff never happened to because I am me and it did.

Here I stand. My human vessel with its scorecard of joy and pain. I am her. I am whole. I am also still that pure spirit and so are you, whatever has happened. You are that incorruptible, beautiful, pure, peaceful spirit.

We often create a huge resistance to allowing our traumas, emotions and our scars to exist. Let alone realising the extensively beneficial spiritual guidance they can offer us. We push them away. Not only because they are painful but because we are constantly bombarded with images, film, and words that convince us that perfection and happiness are achievable if we just work harder. If we spend more money and of course, eradicate those scars, flaws and imperfections.

So, we resist. We resist being our perfectly flawed, naturally imperfect, beautifully scarred selves. We resist filling our aura to the absolute outer brim with who we really are, in case we don't fit in. Or in case we are punished or ridiculed for it. This is especially, but not exclusively, true for women and the generational trauma that we carry at the hands of the longstanding patriarchy. This resistance blocks our ability to fully heal, to reach our magnificent potential and to breathe!

Yes, you know that shallow breathing you catch yourself doing? When you suddenly remember to take a really long deep breath because it's been so long since you took one! (I'll wait while you take a deep breath. And another one...... ready?) That shallow breathing is often resistance. It can be holding back from letting go because letting go might feel like no longer having an excuse not to shine. It can be denying your true self. It can be shrinking in many, many different ways, because of fear. Because of shame. Because of being told you're too much or not enough.

Sometimes we turn away from healing because we're scared of the pain. When we breathe deeply, we feel and see the pain. When we quieten our minds, we are often confronted with all we have buried and the silence can be deafening. It can scream at us. It can plead with us. Or it can manifest physically or mentally - or both- in dis-ease.

We may get glimpses of what we need to go through to heal, and subconsciously our mind makes up a thousand reasons why we can wait. Suppressing grief, sadness and trauma causes so much more damage than the cause itself.

Take four really, really deep breaths. Ask yourself, "Am I being honest about my healing journey?"

Subconscious work and shadow work are, in my experience, where the majority of the work needs to take place in order to fully heal. We can consciously be aware of changes we need to make and why, but with the best intentions in the world, significant lasting change is only possible when the subconscious is accessed and retrained. I am still learning about working on my subconscious through reading, talking, listening and daily practice of mindfulness, repetitive affirmations and actions.

My ongoing personal awakening has really been about slowing down enough to hear, feel and see the patterns of my life and my mind. Instead of a constant repetitive reel of patterns that knock me about, instead of them controlling me, I'm learning to take back control. To see and understand them and their effects. To improve and increase the positive patterns and intercept and retrain the negative ones.

A conversation I had with my eldest daughter recently about revisiting some of her painful experiences made me think about an analogy. I said, "You know when you're reading a book and you suddenly think, "wait, what? Hang on a minute, how did we get here, have I missed something?" Then you flick back a few chapters to a bit you didn't read properly, that didn't quite register properly. Then suddenly the present makes much more sense and you can carry on with the story with a better, fuller understanding of what's already happened. Well, that represents life. Some chapters of our lives we don't fully process or experience. But we don't want to go back and look at them because they're painful or intensely traumatic. We reach a point where we think "what the actual hell is going on?" Certain circumstances or behaviours keep repeating themselves and we have no idea why. But when we do take the time to reflect on the source of them properly it becomes much easier to understand our present patterns and how to change them."

For me, looking within myself, acceptance, awareness, forgiveness, compassion and above all, love -of and for myself and others- have all been essential in feeling a sense of stability and peace no matter what happens. Embracing the spiritual richness and depth trauma can offer me.

I'd like to finish with a poem I wrote earlier this year. I feel it captures the need for us to accept all that is, so that we can move on in healthier, more spiritual ways. So that we can appreciate a more non-dualistic perspective, which in turn, helps us feel whole and capable of anything we set our minds to.

It's called 'As It Is'.

As It Is

Someday all shall be well.
But, more importantly,
All is well.
Right now.
As it is.

This life.
With all its joy and strife.

This year.
With ALL its love and ALL its fear.

This day.
With its speed and its delay

This hour.
With its raging storms and its gentle flowers.

Just as it is.
All is well.
This moment we live to tell.
Its Yin and Yang
Its heaven and hell.

With its highs and lows,
Ebbs and flows.
Its yes and its no
Its dull and its glow

This life.
This learning.
God knows.
We suffer, only when this moment goes,
Unfelt...
Unwitnessed...
Unnoticed...

Wishing life was different
Instead of as it is.

As our minds dash to and fro'.
Seeking solace.
In places where life does not exist.

In the future.
In the past.
In our phones.
With a loved one who passed.
Such a long list.

Adrift in the vast world of material things.
Ambushed by thoughts and feelings
So far from just being.
The truth is missed.

The thing is this...

Happiness and pain,
Go together
That's the way it is.

They need each other.
Like players in a game.
Like sunshine and rain.

Whether we engage or abstain.
The balance remains.
That's the way it is.

Only truly in the moment,
Is the truth so plain.
Only we have the power.
To lose or gain.
Trust this.
But we have to really feel.
WHATEVER is there.
If we dare.
Or our lives will be in vain.
Lost in the mist.
All is well.
Right now.

As it is.

Emma is 49, has 3 children, a granddaughter and lives in Leeds. She is an artist, writer, photographer, film maker, community event organiser, DJ, gardener and has a passion for philosophy, nature and truth. She has recently graduated with a BA Hons degree in Fine Art and continues to work in her community and beyond, bridging art and wellbeing to help empower as many people as possible.

She is an advocate for love, creativity and wellbeing and believes healing is possible for anyone who is ready and willing to do the inner work. She also fights for equality regardless of differences.

Her Artist name is Bliss Brown. If you wish to work with or reach out to Emma you can contact her via email at:

blissbrownart@yahoo.com or visit

https://linktr.ee/blissbrownarts to see some more of her work.

Mindful Reflections
Rebecca Brothers

I had just finished a zoom call- well a job interview actually and I found myself reflecting. I smiled to myself as I barely recognised the confident, chatty person who had conducted herself well during the interview – from the quiet, shy, timid girl who would go bright red and hated reading out loud in English lessons.

So, here's where I try to describe what made the difference, and in doing so, offer some words of wisdom.

Someone saw the potential in me and pushed me well out of my comfort zone. Now, when I look back, I can totally relate to and agree with the statement 'growth happens outside the comfort zone' - as this is where my career started. Without this push, I would not have the career I have today. And ironically, as I write this, I have taken the conscious decision to push myself out of my comfort zone with a new job and to leave my current employer of 15 years. It's safe, easy and comfortable in the comfort zone, hence the name. If you don't push yourself forward every once in a while, then you don't grow!

"Believe in yourself. Because if you don't, then nobody will". This was the feedback given to me by a colleague over ten years ago. To say I didn't take kindly to this feedback at the time is an understatement. I was quite hurt by it and it fuelled my apprehension about being quiet and introverted. The colleague who said it to me was of course, outgoing, chatty and it was no problem for her to voice her opinions. However, she was absolutely right! You have to believe in yourself and have that inner self confidence, which is not always easy. I battled with being an introvert well into my 30s. Always thinking there was something the matter with me, and always being told in every review "be more assertive", which was absolutely easier said than done!

Embrace who YOU are. Don't always compare yourself to those that are more outspoken – and I know this is difficult as they are the people who are always showing and speaking up. Surround yourself with trusted, close friends and believe me, you will have the best conversations.

My final reflection is to find something that nourishes you and helps you out in times of stress. At the beginning of the covid pandemic, I was re-introduced to Mindfulness. Something I had heard lots about, but wrongly thought was just another word for meditation. Learning more on this topic helped me realise I was totally overwhelmed – working from home, harder than ever, when much of the UK was in lock down.

Mindfulness has made such a difference to me. It really came to me when I needed it and I'm so passionate about it. I have built up my practice and continue to learn about it. It really helps you become more aware of your thoughts, and then act upon them. It has undoubtedly helped me through some tough times; the loss of my fur baby, defusing challenging arguments, has helped me react differently to situations. It generally helps me feel better, calmer and gives me clarity of mind. I honestly don't think I would be the same without it. So why not try it, or find your something that works for you, that is positive and nourishing. Find that thing that helps you.

Rebecca Brothers:

https://www.facebook.com/wellnessrebeccaanne/

http://linkedin.com/in/rebecca-brothers-73b300220

Becoming
Jan Muse

My Spiritual Awakening has been a lifelong journey. A series of lessons, of chapters, of being, or not being!

Searching for my true Soul purpose. The big question, why am I here?

My life, like so many others has had its fair share of heartbreak. Dark lonely nights of the soul.

Alone, frightened, battered and bruised. I experienced Homelessness, Addiction, Rape, abuse, eating disorders, toxic relationships.

But one thing is for sure. Even in those darkest of times. I never gave in. Somehow my heart and soul knew there was more to life. I was separated from my daughter due to domestic abuse. The fight to have her back in my life was my driver, propelling me forward.

I could have easily given up and ended it all. Believe me I tried. My heart yearned to hold her again. It is said, when we experience the depths of the bottomless pits, that the light shines brighter if we can catch a glimpse of it at the end of the proverbial tunnel. This light for me was in my daughters' eyes.

I held on tightly to my blessings, hidden in the burdens. Accepted and embraced all that life hurled at me. Treated every challenge as a gift, to learn and grow.

Yes, I have felt like a victim at times. Because, in truth I was. A victim of circumstances, elicited by others and more importantly, by my own hand. Yet, there was no power there for me. Playing the blame game, unwilling to accept my part in each process.

In truth, this victim mentality, held me back. Chained me to the damming energy of helplessness, which only served to disempower and distract me from becoming my True self.

I hid behind my fears. Spent my days people pleasing and longing for acceptance. Desperately craving love and connection with others.

I ignored my own needs, presuming that others would love and accept me if I was kind and helpful, like the good girl I was always expected to be. Forever there at the drop of a hat.

For a while, this strategy worked for me. Or so I believed. Although, time and time again, I would feel let down by others, for them not recognising my needs! Some even turned against me, dragging me back to feelings of uselessness, unworthiness, guilt and despair.

Why would anyone be aware of my needs when I pretended I was ok; projecting myself as that strong woman that everyone turned to?

The truth was, I did not value myself. In fact, I did not even know or like myself. I was disconnected from me, from source. The more I focused on others, the more I drifted away from my inner light, my own soul, my own heart. I avoided my fears like the plague, neglecting myself, feeling unworthy, longing for change, but not knowing how to initiate a new way of being.

I read books, studied many different spiritual paths to enlightenment. I constantly looked outside of myself for redemption and forgiveness. All to no avail. Naturally, I had small glimpses of truths and learned a lot along the way. The fear was real, it kept me separated from myself and others. I was thwarted with ill health. IBS was a constant companion. I continually experienced health conditions, that stopped me moving forward. Affirming to myself, I was safer living on the edge of society. I had test after test by Dr's and hospital. Praying for some relief.

This approach got me nowhere. I was offered medications that only masked the real roots of my problems. Thankfully, I realised I was creating some of these illnesses myself to avoid any more pain from exterior sources. If I continued to hide, I was safe. Safe? Yes. Happy? No.

"Fear, you kept me safe from rejection.
I found a strange comfort, in your embrace.
You smothered my feelings of not being enough.
Kept me captive in a desolate place.
Trauma, I pushed you deep down inside me.
I was strong and I knew I'd get by.
I was existing, always striving, not living nor thriving.
And behind closed doors, I would cry.
I knew that I had to make changes,
A feeling inside so strong.
An innate knowing there was more to life for me.
My awakening had begun."

Slowly, I began to realise that to access healing and freedom from fear, to find the ability to live in wholeness and happiness existed within myself. Naturally, this realization created even more challenges.

For the Seekers path for truth can be truly terrifying. I was so out of touch with myself, I had to dig much deeper within than I ever imagined. Constantly facing layers of emotional trauma. I needed help but had no idea where or who could assist me.

Then, 25 years ago, I attended a local Mind, Body, Spirit event. I listened to the speakers, in awe of their confidence and knowledge. Feeling incredibly inferior. It was here, I discovered Reiki. My soul sang, my heart opened (just a little)- I began to Trust (a tiny bit).

Slowly, I began to let down my boundaries. It was raw and hit me like an overwhelming Tsunami wave of my suppressed emotional self. Bubbling to the surface, gushing, crashing, and wiping all feelings of stability in one fail swoop.

Yet I was not alone. I was held and loved by a higher force. The source of pure love. Of Oneness. Of belonging. I was not alone. I recognised instantly that Reiki could be what I had been looking for. My liberator and saviour.

"Softly, she whispered
In a voice I could barely hear.
My heart and soul reached out.
Listen close my dear.
It's time!
"Time for what?" I asked the voice
Rise up and face your fears!

Journey within and find yourself
Shed those sacred tears
Know thyself, Love thyself
Give thyself permission
Begin to heal, to love to live.
Move yourself into position".

I Moved!

My transition to becoming began to take a promising shape.

With Reiki holding me I started to face my shadow. The sinister, unowned, unconscious, unloved parts of myself. The ugly, suppressed aspects of my being, my worst nightmares. All the qualities I had been instructed by society, that were wrong and forced to suppress.

Here I found my battered Soul. My Inner child, my wounded warrior. Hidden amongst these things were the good parts of me. The successful me, the confident me. The me that I thought was unworthy. Concealed within a false sense of security.

Oh, what a mess I was.

Picking over my stories, observing, and examining myself through new Reiki eyes. I discovered, I was responsible for my own well-being, my conscious choices, I began to call my power back to me.

My soul began to speak, prying open my mind, allowing me to release the old stories, like a snake shedding its skin that no longer fits. I started to see my own and other's reality in a new light.

I discovered that others were hiding too. That we all have our demons to face. That if I engaged with myself, eventually I would become the person I was born to be. Whoever she was.

I started spending more time outside, learning about herbs, flowers, and trees. Being one with all of Nature.

"Mother Nature, you welcomed and accepted me.
As a child of the Earth, of your own.
Your faith in me, surpassed what I felt I deserved
Sweet Maiden, Mother, Crone.
I witnessed seasons come and go,
Felt them coursing through my veins.
Sweet sacred life was shown to me.
I was becoming whole again.
The tides within began to turn,
A flame ignited in my being.
Fresh air filled my lungs with every breath

Mother Nature, your love became my Healing.
Onwards and upwards you carried me,
I listened with great intent
Swiftly I became much stronger
I began my life's ascent"

With Reiki and Mother Nature by my side, my heart full of gratitude for my learnings, wove their way into my everyday living.

The colours around me seemed brighter, food became delicious, rather than a necessity.

My heart was not as shattered and torn. I attended Reiki shares where I was loved and appreciated. Shamanic gatherings that fulfilled my Spirit.

I became increasingly aware of my soul's mission. My experiences and the knowledge I had gained meant I could really and truly help others. There was to be no self-sacrifice, no people pleasing, no neglecting myself.

Each morning, I practised my Reiki meditation, walked barefoot on the grass, counted my Blessings, and connected to Mamma Earth.

Singing "What's up" by 4 non blondes at the top of my voice.

The lyrics really resonated with me, I identified with those four strong women. They seemed powerful, yet vulnerable with their words. I got it!

Music has always been a huge part of my life. Bringing memories of my dad whistling along to radio 1 on a morning, of my first love, of happy holidays, my first grandchild. So many precious, gifted moments in time. Marked with a song that touched my heart and mind.

Music has played an enormous part in my healing; its very design is to entice the listener to feel emotion. There's nothing quite like playing a favourite song, singing and dancing wildly.

Shifting and releasing blocked and stagnant energy, I found that dancing reduces levels of cortisol; our main stress hormone and increases our happy hormone, dopamine. I love to dance. Despite being pulled out of dance classes by my Mum at the age of six and being told I was as "graceful as a baby elephant." A label I carried most of my life.

At the ripe old age of 55 I joined a Burlesque Troupe. A Sisterhood of women, facing our fears. Acknowledging the difference in our body shape, size and age.

During my first appearance solo on stage, I heard my mum's voice, reminding me I wasn't good enough.

Standing in the wings I was physically shaking; my heart was racing. Flight, Fight or Freeze? I felt sick to the bottom of my stomach. But I was determined. I would not let myself or fellow dancers down.

I lifted my face to the sky and said "Mum, this one is for you".

I walked out on stage to my music and the cheers of friends and family in the audience. It felt surreal, like I was dreaming. Like I was in some liminal space. Three minutes and 48 seconds later, it was over. I curtsied to the clapping and cheering crowd. I walked off stage and cried. Part relief, part pride. I did it. I had beaten years of being told I wasn't good enough to dance. I will remember that feeling forever and I continue to perform any chance I get. I faced my fears and did it anyway.

"Standing in the wings of a waiting stage.
Palms sweaty, my heartbeat racing.
In corset and stockings, covered in bling.
Glamour disguising the fear I was facing.
I heard my music intro; the Compere said my name.
I strutted my stuff, feeling free of all shame."

I did it!

One thing I always believed was that boundaries meant restriction! I have learned that making healthy boundaries has, in fact, set me free. I took a good look at where I was restricting myself. Due to trauma and social conditioning. I listened to how I spoke to myself, checking for words like 'I can't', 'I should', 'I shouldn't' and 'I must'. But more importantly, I took stock of when and why I said yes to others and when it really wasn't really in my best interest. It was hard at first as this was a lifetime habit. But the more I said no to others, the more I said yes to me. The more empowered I felt, the less stressed I became. I found I had choice. Choosing what was best for me was not a selfish act, as I had been led to believe. I didn't feel guilty or embarrassed.

I discovered my true friends stayed with me as I began to say no. Other relationships and friendships fizzled out, and although initially I felt some sadness, I also found those were exactly the people who were draining my energy. One-way friendships that I was allowing. When they realised I wasn't jumping in to save them, they found someone else who would.

What an eye-opener and confirmation this was for me. It felt amazing that I was taking care of my needs first. I was becoming Me.

The TRUE Divine me. The shining part of me that is within us all, whom we can all find if we choose to dig deep into our shadow. To accept all of ourselves, faults, and all. To live in and from our spiritual heart, that connects us to the Source of Higher Love. Unconditional Love.

Here I found Love and acceptance. I was the one. The one I was looking for. The one who saved me.

"I am darkness, I am light.
I am grounded, I take flight.
I am the hottest summer day,
And the coldest winter night.
I am the deepest of oceans,
The highest of stars.
I'm a little bit Venus,
And a little bit Mars.
I've been a leader,
I've been led.
I've been starving,
I've been fed.
I've been shallow,
I've dived deep.
I'm Awake,
But I still love sleep.
I've lived on the streets,

I've slept in a bed.
I've been stone cold sober,
And way out of my head.
I've lost count of the times,
That I've almost died.
And counted my blessings,
Each time I've survived.
I've been loved, I've been hated.
I've been a saint, and X rated.
I'm a mother, a grandma, a sister, a wife.
I've been a loser and a winner,
I'm pro-choice and pro-life.
I've stood up for freedom,
I've sat down for peace.
I've rocked against racism,
Been beat by police.
And it's all within me,
And it's within you.
If we open our hearts,
We will find common Truths.
We all have our stories,
We all have our song.
We all need each other,
For us to move on.
It's not black or white,
It's not that or this.
It's above us, below us,

Between and betwixt.
The Air that we breathe,
The Earth under feet.
The fires in our bellies,
The waters so deep.
So, lets unite people,
Love and support one another.
Stop judging and dividing,
Let's work with our Mother.
We are Earth-keepers,
We chose to be here.
Hold on to your hearts,
And release all your fears.
Let's hold each other up,
Let's all dare to dream.
After all brothers and sisters,
We are all Kings and Queens.
I am Becoming.
I am becoming Crone.

Jan Muse had always been interested in the natural world. At an early age *she realized she had a strong connection with nature and spirit.*

She is blessed to live in the beautiful Peak District, where she has had the opportunity to learn much more about what Mother Nature provides for us.

Most of the workshops and training she offers are based on natural healing. Whether this be energy work, cacao and plant spirit medicine, Reiki, herbs and an all manner of natural magic.

She also has her own range of flower essences, made at her home in the Peak District.

Jan has been a Reiki Practitioner since 1997 and has built up her holistic studies and qualifications over the years, to ensure everyone she comes into contact with has the best tailor-made experience.

Jan believes relaxation and connection with nature is the key to better health. In fact, it is said that around 75% of illness in the U.K. could be attributed to stress.

Jan believes that it is important for her clients to receive a service that empowers them to move forward and offers tools which enable self-healing.

Her workshops, treatments, ceremonies and training are available online and in person.

magicalmuse60@gmail.com

www.magicalmuseholistics.co.uk

https://www.facebook.com/groups/764566414320188/?ref=share

Wanderlust
Swey Jitti

She ran through the woods,
She swam all the seas,
She found comfort
When facing the breeze

The winds were in favour
Everytime her sails let loose
For they found comfort
In their new-found truce

She climbed up the peaks
Of mountains
never heard or seen
For she found comfort
In the truth of the steep

The snow settled on the shores
Of long islands
forgotten by all
But they found comfort
Knowing soon
there will be fall

She watched the leaves
turn in colours
To the rhythm
of the seasons
For she found comfort
Knowing there is reason

In the sun that sets
And the moon, that shines
They find comfort
Knowing the world
they see over
is absolute divine

She knew her soul
A wanderlust
Yearning to roam the earths
But she found comfort
In all the memories
That once she lived
For she knew
What she had
Were treasures
Far more worthy
Than silver or gold.

Swey Jitti
https://linkpop.com/sweyjitti

A Song to Sing
Jemma Rosenthal

Journeying the Healing of my Mind

During this writing process I had a conversation with my mum, I was having some writer's block and my mum had offered to help. I asked her to share her wisdom, what she's learnt over the years, and this is what she said:

"When I was younger, I tended to compare myself to others, thinking everyone was better than me. That was a judgement. I never listened to people when they praised me. Often, when you are stressed or down it's because you can only see the bad. There's good and bad in everything, it's not about whether someone else is good or bad, it's really about seeing the positives in life.

You can't change the past. You've only got the present. If you're going over and over the past, there's nothing you can do about it anyway.

If you see someone going through a hard time, if you judge that person, it doesn't help. You have to listen and validate them. You don't have to agree with them, but what I've learnt is to be non-judgemental and validating.

The other thing I learnt, initially from the first therapist I had, is called Behavioural Activation. I always feel better when I've achieved something. That means you've done something positive, whether it's helping the children I work with or it's doing the washing up, anything. Whatever it is, you're working towards something. When you're working against, you are ruminating, judging the past. Giving yourself a break is important; your food, sleep, you need that for your sanity as well. To take care of yourself and others.

3 things I've learnt to help live a peaceful and happy life:

- Looking after yourself
- Being non-judgemental and validating other people (not necessarily agreeing with them)
- Being open to ideas and thinking outside the box

Another thing I've learnt, from the DBT course (me and my parents took a Dialectical Behavioural Therapy course) and from you as well (aw thanks mum!), is being aware of your emotions. Sometimes you need to stop. Wait till you've calmed down, not rush into things. 'The 5 Senses' mindfulness exercise and in CBT, 'The Worry Tree' have helped me. Sometimes you can sort a problem out, or you can book a time to come back to it later, and sometimes you can let it go."

I believe we are all born with wisdom within us. As children, we were naturally wise. Doing what made us happy. Expressing our emotions when we felt angry, joyful or sad. Keeping close to the ones who nurtured us, and brought us warmth and food. Babies are so close to the memory of the mother's womb, yet as adults, we forget this innate connectedness. Turning instead to an ego-made self, a fabricated reality of separation. Separation then became such a natural 'fact' of life, that the memory of where we came from almost ceases to exist. Only a faint glimmer of the spark of creation is left. A grand illusion was created instead to uphold the entire belief systems and structures of the world. Fear was born. Love, seemingly a mere fantasy or a far-off dream, only to be experienced in moments, then to be taken away.

When I was studying for my performing arts degree (and really throughout my career in the arts and coaching), I felt under an incredible amount of drive to perform my best constantly. The amount of anxiety and internalised pressure to 'be the best' caused me to panic if I couldn't. One time, I decided to call my friend to tell her the problem.

"I'm not sure I can do this," I said. "Well, maybe I can, I'm pretty good at solving problems, yeah maybe I can do this." Then I talked myself out of it. "No, I'm not good at things, I'm useless." I'm paraphrasing here as I have no idea of what the actual problem was that I was anxious about. This is largely irrelevant in the context here, the point is, I was not trusting myself. I was in fear.

"You know," she said, "you do this a lot. You find the positives, then you talk yourself out of it." Suddenly, I was aware of the trees above my head, swaying in the wind, the bench I was sat on, holding me up and the people walking past the busy park.

"Yeah...," I pondered slowly, "that's true." As I put down the phone, I paused. "Why do I do this?" I thought. I recognised my habitual patterns of thinking, and became aware that I was, in fact, identifying with this thinking! Noticing this, I became, instead, the observer. These were the initial stages of awareness. In that moment, I learnt that my thoughts were controlling how I was seeing the world. I saw that I could change this. I made a decision to change.

A few months later, sat on the sofa in my London flat, it's 2012. I was having a conversation with another friend. "It has not been an easy time recently," I told him. "I've been feeling quite down and things seem confusing. I want to communicate more but am finding it difficult to express. I've started reading A *New Earth by Eckhart Tolle*, and this has been helping to change my way of thinking about it. Being in the now." Talking was comforting. My friend then tells me of a tribe that he once heard of, that were brought up to believe that the other is a part of their own self. "Of course, this is really difficult for us to live like this," he reasons, "as we haven't been brought up like that." I froze on the spot, as a deep profound stillness occurred, suddenly aware of the sofa I was sat on.

Gobsmacked.

My awareness suddenly went to the window and the curtains, and then out beyond the windows, past the trees and even further out. "It's true!" I exclaimed. "We are all one!" To even put into words the profoundness of what I was feeling in that moment is difficult. However, all I can say is, I realised that this moment was, and is, all there ever is. I felt connected to everything and everyone. No separation.

After having this awakening of the interconnectedness of all things, it was like something shifted. Synchronicities started to happen and I was being drawn to different places and people. I met people who had also been reading Eckhart Tolle's books, and experienced similar things to I had.

One time, on one of my walks in the area of Crouch End, where I was living, I came across a sign: Meditation Class. "Wow," I thought, "this is for me! What a coincidence I should find this on my journey of awakening." So I sat down in the class as the teacher starts to tell us about how to awaken. "It takes many years of dedicated meditation to reach enlightenment, even some people who've spent years don't reach it."

"It has happened to me," I said, loudly and clearly as I sat in the middle of the rows of chairs. "I have awakened." Everyone looked at me and my face was now slightly flushed, the teacher sympathetically repeated her point. "No, this is something else, enlightenment happens after many years of study and training." "Mmm," I wondered, "is she correct? Am I not awake? Could this be right?" I sat for a little longer and enjoyed the meditation. Then I started to feel angsty, wanting to move. "I'm leaving now," I expressed, and got up and left the meditation class. "I don't have to stay there," I thought, "I'm free. This world is an illusion. I'm enlightened anyway."

I carried on walking until I reached a small restaurant. There were dirty plates and things on the tables so I started to pick them up and take them to the waiters. "I want to help," I think. "Why should it be always up to the staff to do this? Why are there these silly rules constricting us from being of service?" "Thanks," says the waiter, "that's very kind of you to help." We exchanged smiles. Once again I felt the urge to leave. "I'm leaving now," I announced. So I left.

As I went out onto the now dark, yet lit streets, I felt a slight uneasiness. "Am I ok? Am I going mad? Is this a dream? It feels so strange and lucid. What's going on with my behaviours?" Intense fear arose. All that had been repressed suddenly became manifested into not only a lucid dream, but a nightmare. I was vulnerable in this state. Objects started to become fearful. A plant was terrifying. A ruler was a symbol of oppression by a fearful world out to get me. People looked different. Their eyes were bigger. Either they became intensely beautiful or they appeared monstrous. Lines on faces were etched almost as if I was witnessing in a cartoon, beyond 3D. My senses had widened, I was able to pick up on such nuances of moments, other moments disappeared completely.

I decided the best course of action would be to travel back to my home town of Sheffield and stay with my family, where I put on some films, only to realise the films had now finished. "Wait have we watched the film?" I asked my sister. "I don't remember seeing any of it."

Eventually, I was hospitalised.

I later had a conversation with a work therapist who explained to me the thin line between psychosis and spiritual awakening. I started to understand what had happened. I learnt that the mind can only tolerate a certain amount of anxiety/pain, before it breaks. There was no other option but to awaken to a deeper dimension. This was something I had no education or awareness on how to cope with or handle this type of sudden change in perspective. In order to calm the mind, I needed support and reassurance. I needed healing and understanding.

I now since have been to many more meditation classes, and practice mindfulness as a daily routine. I've realised that both myself and the meditation teacher were correct and incorrect. Yes I had awakened. And, yes, it does takes years of spiritual dedication to be enlightened, I did need to do a lot more meditation, and still do. Yet, paradoxically, I am always and have always been, awake. We are always here. Always here, always now. As the spiritual book *A Course in Miracles* helped me to understand, awakening is always instant. Time/space reality doesn't reflect our true self, yet it always has the potential to, should we wish to see it. As for the truth of how awake or unawakened you or I really am? Can we really be the judge of this?

I knew in order to heal I couldn't do this alone. Before this had happened writing songs was something I did all the time, so surely I could do this. It wasn't easy to start with. The pills I was on dulled my experience of the world, I had little motivation, and I slept a lot. Clumps of my hair falling out onto my hands, bloated face, I felt like my sense of who I was disappearing.

One day, my sister came into the room with her guitar to cheer me up! She shared with me a song she'd written, "I wrote it for you and mum," she said. I was so surprised and grateful that I suddenly felt more myself again! We wrote some songs together and then I was now ready to do one again myself. I went to the keyboard and started to play some eerie notes, as a bass line appeared.

"Thoughts racing as I'm lying in bed, like thunder bolts in my head, I can't sleep my heart beats." I wrote a full song.

The chorus is a declaration of my dedication to recovering. "I'm taking back control of my mind, of my mind." (Now a song called *Of Their Minds* and now is done from a 3rd person story of various people, all in recovery to heal their minds).

What I learnt from this is the deep desire I had to heal was so strong and my love for music and song writing could play a part in this. And that having my sister reflect to me this love for music and a determination was what I needed. This was so potent. I knew I had what it took to get myself through this. I knew my mind had the capabilities to use what I loved to support this journey.

Another thing I did was I went to as many therapists and courses that I could. One time, I was sat on the couch at my therapist's house. Her own art on the walls, she was an artist. I admired this, being a creative myself. This session, we were doing inner child healing. Integrating my adult self to care for my younger self. Popping out from behind the door the dog comes in. Sitting beside me and snuggling up. "Do you want the dog out?" my therapist asks. "No, no," I said, "it's ok." Smiling, I started to feel an overwhelming relief come through as I released tears and let go. "Wow," I say. My hands felt calmer in the fur. "The dog really helped me release my emotions." "They tend to pick up on when we need comforting the most. They sense it," she explained.

What I learnt from this experience is how much we need dedicated time to process things. As well as the healing power of connecting with animals. The presence they hold is profound.

Embarking on a wonderful journey of awakening, it is important to be patient with ourselves and do the inner work. If there is truly only one of us here, how can we allow this reality to guide us? Or is it too frightening a concept to fathom that love could be real? Not only real, but eternal and unchanging. Who would we be without our own fear of the world? Who is there to blame if the person who hurt you is but your very own self, a projected aspect, hidden and dismissed, only to be seen as a reflection back at you, on a mirror screen of reality? Where are judgements when the only ones we are judging, are ourselves? Are we so *Afraid of Love* (own song reference intended ;)) that we could not even grasp such a reality to be true?

It is my hope that we can learn to see the other as ourselves, and to share what we love. Through my journey, and working with others, I've seen so much joy and healing happen. When we allow ourselves to let go of fear and return to a state of joy; of harmony with life, wholeness with ourselves, wholeness with the earth, wholeness with each other- we all have a song to sing.

Best-selling Co-author of The New Woman- Stories of Kintsugi experience and also featured in Treasure Stories of Lockdown; Founder of Creative Hearts,

Jemma Rosenthal graduated with a first degree in Professional Dance and Musical Theatre at Urdang Academy, London.

After a spontaneous spiritual awakening and years of deep healing practices, she is now a trained Life Coach and Reiki level 2 Healer. She has acted in short films, has released her own music and recently directed her video 'Everything is You'. BBC Radio Sheffield described her voice as 'Angelic'.

She also co-hosts Find, Tell, Share: The Storytellers Podcast. Jemma is determined to use her voice to support others on this awakening journey.

The Bird No Longer Sings Alone

Sara K Jackson

We lay on our backs in this disconnected world.

Feeling the earth deceive us as we watch the movement of clouds.

The sun appears nervous.

We can feel him but he has yet to emerge.

The noise of traffic dissipates, as my ears grab hold of the sound of a single singing bird.

And this morning I recall myself

washing reality down the sink.

The decay of yesterdays.

Their decomposed opinions I devoured when I was weak.

Removing the stones from my shoes.

Shaking the phantoms out of my sheets.

That night was black.

I recalled past events.

Trying to connect a line to a jagged edge.

Nursing a heart that had poured its last drop.

No balance. No cooperation.

Negative shades in the backdrop.

I still gave with little awareness of knowing how to stop.

What use is a heart if not to give?

The present day speaks to me -

RECIPROCITY

Seeing my inner value and worth.

So now I tune my frequency to what I want to attract.

Negativity, I've learnt to subtract.

Letting go of those, that place a hand over my mouth when I speak, in fear of hearing an opposition to what they think.

My words have substance and want to live.

It is ironic, how silence holds the most noise.

Feelings imprisoned by fear as they aren't functional in the world we live.

But they exist.

So I don't ignore what should be felt.

Honesty drags me through the remains of uncertainty to a place called Peace.

I smile, as a lay with a heart that mirrors mine.

The waves of thoughts easily intertwine.

Balancing the scales.

Flavouring my inner universe with sweet extracts

Acceptance.

Friendship.

What a beautiful thing.

And now I hear that bird,

no longer sings alone.

Instagram: Skjacksonart

Quote by S.K. Jackson

"Love doesn't just exist; it is created. Hate doesn't just exist; it is created. And the choice resides in all of us; as we are the creators."

Becoming a Spiritual Warrior
Jennifer McKenzie

I have heard spirituality referred to as nonsense, hippy dippy bullshit, airy fairy stuff, amongst other terms that dilute the power of spiritual practice. Often these terms come from those who do not understand what spirituality is about or have no idea what a spiritual awakening can do to improve their quality of life. Thing is, we are all spiritual whether we want to acknowledge this or not. Spirituality looks and feels different for all of us, but has some common factors, which I am going to talk about in more detail, such as fear, love, connection, being present and surrender.

We are all connected. We are all connected to mother earth too. When we realise this, we become more connected instead of being separated by the ego. When we start honouring our own natural rhythms and living in tune with the cosmos, our quality of life automatically improves. We discover a sense of belonging with a bigger whole, we feel less lonely and isolated and we become more peaceful, harmonious and connected.

Taking time out for spiritual practice and nature rituals reminds us that we are a part of this amazing planet, not apart from it. Nature is one of the best anti-depressants available. Of course, spirituality means different things to different people and there are many paths you can take, above all else be sure to follow your heart and soul, not someone else's.

Here are a few of my learnings and lessons from my journey as a spiritual warrior...

To embark on a path of spirituality, or have the courage to face a spiritual awakening is a pure act of bravery in my humble opinion. It requires you to face fears, become aware of your own subconscious programming and make conscious, sometimes uncomfortable changes, so you can live with more peace and freedom.

I was the weird kid! The one that had shaved half her hair, wore funky coloured tights, Doc Marten boots, had crystals in her pockets, obsessed with the moon and stank of incense sticks. I didn't identify this as spiritual at the time- it was just what I liked and what I was curious about. You would find me outdoors most of the time, up a tree or with animals- I much preferred animals to humans, still do! I was curious about many things. Why people did what they did, who planted that huge oak tree in my favourite park, could animals understand us, and why were grown-ups always lying?!

School and social situations gave me anxiety. They filled me with fear, so I soothed myself with the above- nature, solitude and writing under the moon. I wasn't cut out for rules, sitting still or long days in the matrix. I was born to run barefoot, dance round fires, not brush my hair and be free.

I remember feeling a strong presence around me as a child. I would like to be alone, but I always felt someone, or something was always with me. I was, what is described as, a highly sensitive child. I would literally feel others' emotions in my own body. I somehow knew things that they had never said out loud to me, which seemed to scare some of my friends, but became a bit of a game.

I was bullied at school for being weird. Often adults would deny my reality, get me to conform, tell me I was too loud, say I ask too many questions. This eventually crushed my spirit and led me down a very different and dark path. A path where I no longer trusted my intuition, a path of domestic abuse, addiction, feeling I was never good enough. I partied hard to block out pain, anxiety and fear in the name of calling it fun. Don't get me wrong, most of it was fun, until my life became unmanageable. Being highly sensitive had its perks, but to feel everything so very deeply was a curse to me. So, I began to numb it out with alcohol. It is only on reflection I can make sense of this. After I lost my way and found my light again, after spiritual awakening. Later in life I was told by many of my elders I had a gift. I was a lightworker here to help others.

I would 100% say I am an empath- According to the Oxford dictionary, the definition of an empath is this: *(chiefly in science fiction) A person with the paranormal ability to perceive the mental or emotional state of another individual.*

Spirituality is represented in the media of enlightened people sitting crossed legged on a mountain chanting OM. While this is a wonderful place to be (and in my experience, this comes much later down the line), an awakening can be scary, confusing, and pretty dark at times. please do not let this put you off though, spirituality is beautiful. I have had many dark nights of the soul, but those dark moments taught me so much about myself.

This is an extract from my journal, in addiction:

"In the shadows of the depths of depravity, my soul whispered to me "it's OK, you are going to be OK. This pain is teaching you to be strong, this will make you wiser. You will rise again." The darkness and the solitude became my biggest teacher, here I could really see myself- like really see myself and what I was capable of and what I could survive. It was a necessary suffering to endure so I could truly appreciate the value of life"

Let me break down the awakening for you, in my own words and experience.

The awakening or the initiation may come after a traumatic event or a big change in circumstances. You may feel lost, confused, depressed or highly anxious. Like nothing makes sense anymore. You begin to question the meaning of life and why you are here.

Then you are craving. Seeking deeper connections, deeper meaning - rethinking what you already know, shifts in beliefs- new perspectives. The beliefs that were given to you as a child no longer resonate. You feel like breaking free.

At the next stage, you realise all the answers are already within you. You have a strong urge to grow and learn, beyond the superficial. Your interests and values change as you awaken further.

Then comes the butterfly emerging- transmutation into your true essence of yourself, old patterns are dissolving, you feel more comfortable in your own skin, feeling joyful, excited about what is coming for you.

Spiritual alignment is the final stage - alignment with higher self and the universe. This will be a continuing life journey- seeing the bigger picture, the veil has been lifted. You feel connected and peaceful. Ego death - from I to we. Understanding we are all connected, being in flow and deeply connected to your soul purpose. Confidently showing up as yourself, abundance flowing in love, health and happiness.

The journey can be scary or lonely at first- having a coach or a mentor can be a great support but ultimately the magic and the answers are already within you.

Let's explore some of those feelings.

Fear/Courage

What is fear? Fear is something we learn; we are not born fearful; we learn from mimicking our care givers and from our life experiences. Fear can consume us, or we can choose to feel the fear, tune into our warrior energy and go forth. Fear comes from our core beliefs and is the underlying feeling of many other secondary emotions, such as anger. Emotions are not to be feared but to be leaned into.

When we have the courage to sit with our emotions or speak up for ourselves, even when our voice is shaking- that is courage. Emotions are neither good or bad. They are what they are. The whole spectrum of emotions is normal to feel throughout our lives. Often, we are taught to bypass these uncomfortable emotions and 'just be happy'. This is unhelpful and somewhat damaging for your health as all emotions carry an energy. If this energy is suppressed, it resides in the physical body where it stagnates and manifests into pain, discomfort or even disease. Courage to face parts of us that aren't considered pretty or attractive, for example, jealously. Jealousy highlights where you want to be and is rarely about the other person, merely a reflection of unhealed parts of yourself.

I often refer to myself as a warrior, mainly because of what I have personally been through in my life, survived and faced. Next time fear stops you in your tracks, try thinking 'what's the best that can happen here?' I either try and everything turns out amazing, or I learn that wasn't for me and I do something different. Do it scared! Truth is, we all feel fear- it is how we face it that will help us grow. Owning the fear and reaching out to others for encouragement can really help.

Oneness/Connection

Everything is energy and energy is everything! We are all connected by the invisible force of cosmic deliciousness that is universal life force energy. The planets, mother earth, seasons, animals, plants, people, even objects. Everything we consume carries an energy. Our words, what we watch on TV, see on social media, the people we surround ourselves with. And if you are highly sensitive like me, then your energy reserves will need protecting even more. Pay attention to what feels good. Your energy is sacred. When we are disconnected from our true selves, our energy will feel depleted. I learnt to connect to myself through journaling, writing poems and being in nature. I found these practices wonderfully soothing. I found a tribe of like-minded people that I could connect with and share. Elders that would pass on their words of wisdom. The world began to feel safe again. In those times of loneliness, to protect my energy, I would create healthy loving boundaries. Saying yes to things that light me and no to everything else.

Conscious Change

Becoming conscious and expanding our conscious awareness involves making choices. An average adult makes about 35,000 choices a day- now that is a lot of decisions! How many of those are you aware of? I think most of mine involve deciding what I'm going to eat.

This part of the awakening requires change- conscious change- and by that I mean becoming aware. But how can we change what we are not aware of? On my journey, I became aware I wanted to change. I felt I was outgrowing people and old behaviour patterns. Certain things were no longer fulfilling. I was seeking a different lifestyle away from the chaos of partying. I longed for peace. But I didn't know any different, I didn't know how to change. Change can bring up fear- fear of the unknown. Humans are habitual creatures, so we do the same things repeatedly because it feels safe. We have been wired that way. I was afraid of the unknown. Who was I without the party life? What would I do instead? With the awakening, I was brought back to more of my childlike version of myself. I rekindled a love of nature, running bare foot, letting go of old versions and embracing my true self.

Surrender/Letting go

Spiritual surrender happens when we have come to the point where we're on our knees- totally accepting that we don't really know anything. When we finally understand that, Truth is way beyond our thoughts and beliefs and that there is no way we can figure out any of it. The only thing in the way of the flow has been us, or the person we have been taught to believe we are. No matter how much we try to control our mind, focus our thoughts and all that, all it does is that it keeps the mind busy, thus keeping us away from the present moment.

All these attempts to control will eventually end up in some kind of failure (not that there are any real failures in life, but you know what I mean), and the seeking of solutions continue until true surrender occurs and that often happens when we feel utter defeat and we can't take it anymore. When we're spiritually on our knees waving the white flag of surrender, absolutely exhausted by our own attempts to make life into what we want it to be. Until we stop. One day, the letting go of control and taking it back just have to stop.

I have done this myself numerous times in my own life, until the day came when I declared DEFEAT.

It was November 2015. I'd had enough of the merry go round that was my life...I wanted to get off. My life was a constant battle of me trying to control everything in my life and failing miserably. As you can imagine this was exhausting. My mental health had been spiralling out of control, I was drinking heavily, relationships with family were hanging on by a thread.

I made the decision everyone is better off without me. I decided that I wanted to check out of earth....so I did...I tried to take my life, put an end to it all!!

I survived which I am grateful for now, and was taken to a psychiatric ward where I had a profound Spiritual awakening. I got down on my knees and surrendered. I surrendered control - the fight had become too much! Something shifted in me, I physically felt it. I sobbed and sobbed like I'd never sobbed before. That day changed my life forever. I had a calling to step up into my purpose- to help others. I made a promise I would not give up anymore and I rose up to be a Warrior once again.

That's when my life took a whole other direction, better than I could ever had imagined.

But before that happened, I was drawn back to duality, even if we know that we are one with Life itself. We know because we have tasted it. We know, because we have experienced it, we have seen it, we have lived it. I kept bouncing from one to the other, my spiritual path and my ego self. Between spirituality, clean conscious living and then addiction, fear and control. But still, back to duality at times. (Reverting back to living from the "I" that is separated from the whole, from oneness).

When we work with ourselves and when we build our awareness around what's going on, the path will get easier to manoeuvre. We need to empty our cup completely, let go of painful narratives, identities and the past.

Remember that only the ego does that; while the spirit lives in the Now. So, by bringing ourselves back to this moment, we will find peace, because it's already here. This was like a re-birth. I felt like I'd been given a second chance, I found my purpose in life, I had been given an earth mission to use this painful experience for good. After a while had passed, I felt ready to speak about my experiences. I shared my addiction and mental health journey on many platforms- a journey of survival and spiritual awakening. Someday you will tell your story and it will be someone else's survival guide.

Healing/Love

Healing happens by feeling. By focusing on love. Leading with love and choosing to be compassionate to ourselves at every stage of our journey. I would be horrible to myself but kind to others- does that resonate with you too? My inner dialogue was berating and I'd feel disgusted when I looked in the mirror. I found a book that my Mum had lent me years ago- funny how these things appear when you need them the most. The universe works in powerful ways. The book was how to heal your life by Louise Hay. This book was a catalyst that changed the way I viewed myself and how I started to learn to love myself and the world around me again. Once I accepted who I was, connected with my true self behind the mask, my inner world became more peaceful and so did my outer world.

There is so much beauty in all of us. Not superficial beauty; the beauty of someone's softness, someone's strength, their laugh, their touch, their ability to hold space- this beauty is in you too. Love is everywhere if you choose to feel it, and if you can't see it- be the love. Bring the love into that space. For me, now, I see love and beauty in simple things, like the flowers in my garden, the sound of birds in the morning, the beauty in being kind and not letting my experiences make me cold or bitter.

The continued journey of Awakening

If Spirituality is a path you choose to take, you will experience many awakenings on your journey. It is a continuum of growth. A shedding of layers until you reach joy, inner peace or even enlightenment. Each situation, challenge, relationship, or encounter is teaching you something. Look for the lessons, the blessings, let go of the past and keep bringing yourself into the present. Enjoy the messy, beautiful ride of what we call life!

This is a poem I wrote one night in bed, thinking about life, my journey and fellow warriors I have around me.

I Am a Warrior Woman

You can keep your tiara and high heels
Give me a sword and a horse
For I am a warrior, not a princess.
No-one is coming to save you, dear.
You have to save your damn self.
Set fire to the things that stand in your way
Like fear, self-doubt or worry.
I have withstood test after test
Still I stand, undefeated.
I am now coming for everything they said I couldn't have.

Claiming my power as I rise from the flames
Leaving behind anything or anyone that doesn't serve me in its ashes.
It may look like I walk alone
As you cannot see my army that walk beside me.
My ancestors, my guides, my protectors – come.
Take my hand.
I can see in your eyes
You are a warrior too.

Jennifer McKenzie is a 40-year-old Mum of 4- Nature Lover, Deep thinker, Truth Speaker, LGBTQ supporter.

Jen is the founder and owner of Lunar Spirit Wellbeing Limited. She is a Spiritual Empowerment Coach, Anxiety Therapist, Reiki Master /Teacher, Author, Host of That Inner Voice Podcast and Societal Rebel. Jen also facilitates transformational spiritual retreats.

A spiritual awakening saved her from an unfulfilling life of drug addiction, domestic violence, and self-loathing. Now Jen pays forward her professional and personal knowledge. For the last 6 years Jen has been guiding people just like you through their own awakening journey, so they can overcome deep rooted traumas, fear, anxiety, low self-esteem to create emotional freedom, inner peace and confidently live life on their own terms - putting the proverbial middle finger up to society's expectations of us.

Jen is big into science and spirituality- connecting the mind/body/soul and utilising her 20 plus years of holistic therapy and energy healing practice combined with NLP, DBT, Anxiety coaching, addiction counselling, mindfulness/meditation/sound, releasing breath work and reiki teaching qualifications - this is POWERFUL shiz!!

Find out more and connect with Jen www.lunarspirit-wellbeing.com

The Reawakening
Rachael Lemon

I truly believe there is no 'right' way to be spiritual. You can show up as your playful, quirky, wild, fun, joyous self and still hold impeccable authentic spiritual space in this world.

I've always been spiritual. Other little girls were playing with dolls or plaiting hair and doing makeup; I was in the garden, fields or forest having magical adventures with fairies, trees and animals. I could be found making my own potions from rose petals, curing stings with nettle leaves, wishing on dandelions, casting spells, collecting sea shells, grounded by the sea or river.

I've always felt like I never totally fitted into the conventional 'norm'. A natural empath with the ability to sense, feel and connect with others deeply-extremely perceptive of what's going on in those around me. A dark, inherent humour, fascinated by mystery. Vivid dreamer, drawn to moon magic and its mysterious energy.

As a teen I learned to read tarot and had a vast book collection that spanned the unknown, Wicca, fortune telling, nature, science and murder (trying to understand human capacity for evil rather than practical tips).

I was enchanted with all things supernatural; occultism, paganism and Wicca. I heard stories of how my great aunt was a witch from my grandfather, who was a Christian and didn't approve. Sadly, I didn't get to meet her until I was in my late teens. In reality, she was a renowned healer and medium; leader of the local spiritualist church. I was fascinated by her storytelling and the energy she exuded. Aunt Maud was certainly an inspiring lady and people travelled far to get her healing. I still get told stories by strangers now and she often comes through as a spirit guide when I receive readings.

Such is life, after education, I followed a traditional career path qualifying in pharmaceutical sciences. But I've always been drawn to holistic and alternative therapies- choosing them for myself where possible over conventional medications.

Just as the global pandemic struck the world, I was diagnosed with a rare incurable autoimmune disease. This forced me to slow down and reminded me life's not just to work, no matter how passionate you are about your purpose.

I'm now transitioning from a rewarding professional career in pharmacy, 25 + years in hospital clinical roles, national leadership and most recently, teaching pharmaceutical sciences- to follow a soul led life, that aligns with my spiritual reawakening.

My calling now is to empower, inspire and lead other people to light up their own magic. To facilitate healing, self-love, spiritual nourishment, raised energetic vibration. To enable others to step into their own power and live an authentic happy life, aligned with their soul-purpose.

Finding our magic is the secret to living an inspired life. I believe that there is magic at the heart of all of us beautiful souls, living here on earth. Sometimes we need guidance to find it, by digging deep within, doing the shadow work and spiritually nourishing our souls. Knowing that all the answers are contained within ourselves and when we connect to our own superpower, we are an unstoppable force.

I've always felt strong enough to live life on my own, unconventional terms - even if that means periods of alone time, as I deal with challenges the universe throws in my path. Travelling the rollercoaster of life. I'm finding contentment in nature, surrounded by animals - more so than people! Maybe my spirituality and my intuition are my superpowers, and that's why I always have faith that everything happens for a reason and that one day it will all become clear.

Rachel Lemon
www.lemonaidspiritual.com

How my Garden Grows
Jenny Senior

From very early in my life I knew I had a mission to heal- not just myself but others too.

I was always a giver. Very caring, kind, compassionate and empathetic. I genuinely didn't want others to feel the loneliness I had felt through my own traumatic experiences. I have faced many traumas in my life; sexual and physical abuse, severe mental health issues, excessive drug and alcohol use, toxic relationships- and the most recent trauma of losing my mum, who was my best friend.

In order to deflect from addressing these traumas, I dedicated much of my time looking after others, in both my professional and personal life. I had always worked, had a nice home and managed to achieve qualifications in many areas (after only attending school for 42% of my final academic year)- including achieving a degree in my mid 30's, as a working single-parent, who had just lost her mum. I was often perceived by others as having 'my shit together' (I don't think we ever have it ALL together BUT we can most definitely live a life that is aligned to ourselves, to our soul).

As far as my awakening and spiritual journey goes, I had been interested in holistic and alternative practices for as long as I can remember. However, it wasn't until my relationship with my daughter's father ended (suddenly and catastrophically on my 30th Birthday), that I truly began to explore and embark on this wonderful- but at times a very daunting- path to enlightenment.

Most of my learning and insights early on were self-sought, through Internet research and books. The Power of Now written by Eckhart Tolle, a German spiritual teacher, is a firm favourite of mine and one of the most valuable spiritual books I've read to date. I often listen to his words via the audible app and can quite happily re-read his chapters of my now, very worn, book.

My peers, family, colleagues and ex partners had little interest in 'all things witchy' (a phrase used by an ex to describe my love for exploring more), and so I often felt very alone at times.

I'm writing this chapter hoping some of my words connect and inspire others.

If, like me, you're a working-class lass who feels a little like an imposter at the local yoga group, or the girl who wants to join a meditation group she's stumbled across on Facebook, but feels like she won't fit in, or the new mum who wants to explore a more holistic way of life - PLEASE don't fear the unknown!

Facing your fears will eventually strengthen your soul in ways that will enhance your growth. Trust me when I say this - the universe is open to us all!

So I guess addressing our fears first is where I shall start....

"All negativity is caused by an accumulation of psychological time and denial of the present. Unease, anxiety, tension, stress, worry - all forms of fear - are caused by too much future, and not enough presence. Guilt, regret, resentment, grievances, sadness, bitterness, and all forms of non-forgiveness are caused by too much past, and not enough presence."
- Eckhart Tolle, The Power of Now, (1997).

Fear?

"What am I afraid of?", I asked. "Everything", I replied. And indeed I was afraid of most things.

Yes, I had confidence in some areas of my life- and many people would see a woman who would say how she felt and what she wanted- BUT, the truth was, she always settled for less. Always seemed like she needed validation from others.

I've learnt, throughout this journey, that I really have to work alongside my fears. As a woman, as a mother, as a lover and friend- suppressing my fears has only ever led to bigger fears. When my mum died, the grief I experienced was so soul destroying. It hurt in places I never knew existed. All I wanted to do was to be with her and leave life behind. It was an extremely frightening time. But in the midst of these frightening feelings and overwhelming emotions, I drew strength- I reached out for therapy and continued to grow.

My growth is my garden, and it grew very messy and slowly at first. My garden didn't look pretty it was over grown with weeds. And so, I began to plant my seeds and nurture them the best I could. I don't always tend to my garden daily, but flowers do often bloom. When I started to reconnect with the world after a period of isolation, I met other like-minded women and it became apparent that all of our gardens had weeds.

Some gardens had recently been weeded and their flowers were flourishing in the beautiful sunshine- which made their soul beam brightly. Others had messy gardens like mine, and some were overgrown with weeds (I saw the weeds as fear and trauma). Although it felt a little sad to see the weeds, this discovery was reassuring. It was reassuring to know that each and every one of these women wanted a garden they felt safe in. I learnt that connecting with other women would help my garden grow- it was all part of my healing process.

At first, I was afraid to heal in some respects because all I'd ever known was trauma and turbulent events. I was constantly in survival mode, so to heal was to find some kind of peace- and peace to me was unknown and unfamiliar. I also believed that peace meant being alone, and being alone wasn't something I enjoyed. In fact. I feared being alone so very much. However, as my journey continued, having alone time was really needed and I can now recognise that solitude is a choice we can make and enjoy. I also learnt that peace is certainly not about being alone. It is finding places and people that give you a sense of calmness and tranquillity.

The fear that I once defined as unpleasant and painful actually created spaces for positive changes. I learnt to embrace my fears, nurture them and evolve from them. Some of the most beautiful experiences I have encountered were initially driven by fear.

Fear can close down opportunities, it can stop us from living in our truth. But when we do get a spark of courage, let that courage burn. Let it burn to shine a light ahead, for that is your sign that you're destined to go on. To continue your journey, to experience and connect with the universe, just as it was intended.

When I began working on myself and facing my fears, healing really started to take place.

Often healing is seen as seeking out professional therapy, and for me I did have professional interventions. From the G.P to psychiatrists, from social workers to counsellors. In my time, I've received a lot of professional help and this help isn't to be dismissed, but I also discovered other ways to heal.

My love for writing and reading has been a massive part of my journey. The holding of a pen and scribing words that yearn to be heard gives me so much peace. It's been a way to release the pain and fear, but also it enabled me much needed reflection. A space to remember fond memories of days gone by. Writing, for me, gives me pleasure and I feel honoured that I'm able to share some of my words with others. Writing may not be part of everyone's journey and that is absolutely fine, but if you feel a calling to write, I would honestly give it a go. It doesn't matter if you're writing in a beautiful leather -bound notebook or if you're writing on the envelope of your electricity bill- all that matters is that you're allowing the words to flow from your soul.

As a writer, I found that journal therapy was indeed my best medicine. Journaling daily helped me to really have some time with myself. Some days there would be pages and pages of poetry, reflections and short stories, and on others a few bullet points of randomness.

Each written word had its own value and I began to recognise this and the importance of the fact that a little is better than nothing at all.

As I continued to grow as a woman, I continued to write. I'd take my journal everywhere; to work, to the park, to the beaches in Menorca. It travelled to Florida and captured reflections from a holiday of a lifetime. It also came along to the beautiful Marina in Albufeira- a place I have revisited several times.

I remember one particular day I had gone for a walk in the Portuguese sunshine, and I eventually sat at the side of the shore watching the comings and goings of the boats. I felt blessed and alive. The water was tranquil, the skies so beautifully blue and the golden sunshine embraced my being. And so, I began to write. I wrote with gratitude, love and kindness. I was thankful so much for my time in Albufeira and the wonderful sights I saw.

Being thankful and showing gratitude is an extremely powerful way to reach a higher level of consciousness. It enhances the feeling of being blessed with what we do have, which, in turn, raises our vibration.

I may have seemed alone on that day as people crossed my path, but on that day, I felt a huge connection to the moment. A connection to the world- one that embraced me. I suddenly realised that everything is connected, one way or another.

So here I'd like to touch upon connection, and how it has also been so beneficial to my healing journey. When you feel that you're ready to awaken or to make a transition into your truth, you too may get the urge for connection. Or to discover the meaning of connection and how that looks for you.

Connection has seen me creating some of the most fantastic friendships and being part of communities that have given me a zest for life and an urge to grow.

Forming new connections can often feel daunting. You can be left wondering if you fit in, but let's face it, not one single person fits into the same mould. We are designed to be unique, and by connecting with others, we can find upliftment and support. It isn't just about connecting with other beings; a connection to yourself, discovering and affirming your needs and wants will also help you reach higher truths.

I found meditation, the use of crystals, angel cards and creating my own rituals -such as floral and fruit baths - helped me to connect to myself and my inner child. To create a safe environment to connect to myself, I would prepare my bathroom with candles, rose petals, sliced fruits and aromatherapy oils. I would assess what areas of my energy felt lacking and use the healing properties of crystals. If I felt I needed love to encompass me, then rose quartz would sit beside me. Or if I felt agitated, I would invite my huge calcite sphere to soak with me in the storm, letting its calming energy radiate through the waters onto my skin. I'd often use this time to do my meditations, although in the bathtub they would be short and guided to maintain safety. With sounds of nature playing in the background, I make time to do this once or twice a week. It helps me stay grounded and take a moment's break from this thing we call life.

Life? What is life, we all wonder?! For many, it's going through the motions of age with certain expectations, such as having a job, learning to drive, finding a partner, marriage and children, buying a home-before retiring and eventually passing on. Many of us see that timeline as what life should be like, but in reality for so many of us, that isn't the case. I often struggled with the fact that my life wasn't like this and still isn't. One of my ultimate lessons on my awakening journey is to live in the present moment.

I constantly thought of sadness from my past or longed for a bright and happy future, yet I never focused on the right here and now. I couldn't seem to concentrate on this very moment, but, when I began to practice a little routine, it reminded me of all the things I was grateful for. Once again, gratitude lifted my vibrations.

So, to bring myself back to the now, when I feel stressed, upset or overwhelmed, I gently close my eyes and tell myself I'm here, I'm breathing and I am safe in this very moment. I just spend a few moments concentrating on my breathing.

Of course we may not be able to do that on every occasion, but I've learnt that there are so many occasions we can do that and it safely brings us back to a better frame of mind.

Once I had learnt this, I felt a huge shift in my outlook on life. I began to trust more in myself and the decisions I was making. I also became much more accountable for my own actions. I had the courage to do things alone, but also to connect with people and things that initially felt alien to me.

I was now open to seeing the world from a whole new perspective, a world that I wanted to embrace.

This part of the world had been hidden by my traumas, by guilt, shame and fear. But now I could feel a sea of love, compassion, empathy, kindness that embraced me. I had a soul mission- to sail the beautiful seas. And even when the tides get strong, my soul is still set to sail.

Once again, I'd like to remind the reader it's normal and natural to go through stages in life, of despair. It's OK to feel lost and broken at times, but I would truly urge you to believe in yourself. Set sail and experience a journey of freedom and higher consciousness.

Everyone's journey is different, but it's a journey just the same.

You have the power to keep going on your travels, embrace and enjoy every experience and find the beauty in the changes you seek to make.

And as I've noted here in my chapter, writing is my love. Here are a few words of mine that I hope you read with trust:

If you feel you are about to fall
Be assured the universe has got you
It is here for us all
It's an energy filled with love
Measuring beyond the stars above
Please love yourself completely and
Without fear in your heart
You are brave
You are beautiful
May you never fall apart
The wise woman within you longing to be free
Whispers gently in your ears
Just breathe and let things be

Jenny is a 36-year-old woman and mother of one from Sheffield. She is qualified in various holistic therapies and holds a degree in Professional Practice in Health and

Social Care. She is currently working alongside vulnerable women on several projects.

You can contact Jenny at: jenny.senior/wordsofthewise@gmail.com

The Pulse of Things
Tessa I Richter

Can you hear it,
the breath of water?
Can you hear them,
clouds floating by?
Can you hear
the songs of your soul?

Hear it, see it, touch it...
the pulse of things as they unfold.
the pulse of things and we are one.

Can you see it,
the sound of snow?
Can you see them,
stones growing old?
Can you see
the beauty of your soul?

Hear it, see it, touch it...
the pulse of things as they unfold.
the pulse of things and we are one.

Can you touch them,
the words we spoke?
Can you touch them,
our hidden thoughts?
Can you touch
love at its core?

Hear it, see it, touch it...
The pulse of things as they unfold.
the pulse of things and we are one.

Tessa I Richter
www.oursecretpotential.com

Buadach Beatha (Journey of the Gaelic Soul)

Lorraine Fergusson

"Bless you for your fear, for it is a sign of wisdom" - Yoko Ono

Fear

This four-letter word has held me back so much in my life. I guess I've always felt it from a young age- reinforced by my parents, teachers, society and the media.

However, as a young child, I didn't let it stop me from doing those scary things, like competing in competitions for my dancing, music, drama and sports. It wasn't until later on in my teens, after some traumatic experiences (that included the untimely death of my daddy- a pivotal and influential person in my life), did I let fear control me. This had a knock-on effect for the majority of my teens and younger adult life.

The fear and terror of facing my pain has led me to engage in a number of self-destructive behaviours throughout the years- feeling lost and alone and not able to connect with others in a meaningful way. I had been hurt, abused, abandoned and rejected by those who were supposed to love and protect me. This had clouded my view of the world and made me not trust others' motives. I built huge walls around me to keep everyone out.

Fear has made me play small and not recognise my own, unique potential. It has pushed me into violent and manipulative relationships and convinced me I was unworthy of love. Fear was like a mask I wore, hiding all the beautiful and best parts of myself. However, I always knew something didn't feel right and there had to be more to my life than how I was living it.

After a lot of therapy, both talking and creative, I was able to self-reflect. It was clear I had experienced a lot of heart-ache and pain. This needed to be seen, felt, heard and expressed in order to shift my own perspective and begin living more in line with my truest, authentic self. My inner wisdom was present in my younger years. The one that was kind, patient, loving and courageous. I decided to honour my fear, listen to what it had to say and turn it into my power.

I have learned that fear is always going to be present, but I don't have to feed into it; in doing so gives it more power. I befriend it now, I treat it like a small, scared, vulnerable child. I listen to what it has to say and offer it unconditional love. This acknowledgement and acceptance of fear loosens its grip over me, and it shines a light on those things that need to be felt, seen, heard and healed.

I learned to challenge those negative and limited thoughts. A book that really helped me with his process was Feel the Fear and Do It Anyway by Susan Jeffers. It made me question the validity of what my mind was telling me, by basing it on what I had already achieved in my life so far. It made me focus on the positive. It taught me to weigh up my pros and cons in each situation; to act on it and to celebrate my achievements, however small. Some days, in my darkest times, this was simply being able to shower after a bout of depression that had seen me bed-ridden for days/weeks.

Transforming my fear is a daily practice, it is not something that goes away. However, I get to decide whether I let it hold me back or not. My own innate wisdom, strength and determination guides me- but only if I remain aware of fears.

Recognising my fears and facing them has led me to becoming much more self-aware. I am able to live more in the moment and not get caught up in the old stories I replayed in my head. I began looking within and not without. I found so much peace and freedom in nature; it spoke to me in ways no person ever could. Nature reminded me to find joy in the simplest of things and brings back that childhood wonderment and awe. It makes me feel less alone and part of the bigger picture. It takes me out of my head and into my heart and soul, for that is the place where true growth happens. I became open and accepting of its magic. So, I spent more time there, listening to the wisdom of the trees and the animals. I began my journey inward, to meet my true self.

There have been a variety of things that have aided my awareness, such as meditation, journaling, women's goddess circles, sand play, Connection Cafe, art therapy, kundalini yoga, sound healing, drumming, breath work and ecstatic dance. They led me to the divine and sacred part of myself that was always there, but I had not connected to in many years.

Journaling, in particular, helped to get thoughts out of my head and onto paper. It offered me a direct link to my intuition and inner guidance system. Letting it flow brought me great wisdom and strength. Yoga and dance helped me to focus on feelings and sensations and to move through the difficult, traumatic experiences I had held in my body for so long. This was pivotal in strengthening my awareness.

The goddess women's circles aided me in connecting to my inner feminine; something I had rejected and felt shame for. It softened me and offered a space to be held by other women, who were on the same journey as me. I learnt about goddesses, some of whom came to me in dreams and meditation. The wisdom and guidance they provided brought me out of some of the darkest moments of my life.

These things, combined, gave me the space to gain clarity and to ascertain what was actually true for me; and what was conditioned into me by society. It made me go within and validate myself, rather than look outside of myself for approval. I had tried that and it made me feel lost and confused. I was living how others expected me to, instead of how I needed to.

This awareness helped me to lead from my heart and to place my worth internally, as opposed to externally. To begin to love and accept my body and honour it as my temple. To begin to pursue my passions and follow the natural cycles of life. To speak up more on what I need and to surround myself with people who encourage me. To be more self-accepting and to embrace my imperfections.

Having this new-found awareness made me take the actions of others less personally and it gave me a sense of empathy. I no longer blame

people for how my life was, but took full responsibility for my own choices. This was a difficult process. I don't condone the harmful actions of others, but, it made me see that they were in pain and were disconnected from their true selves. I did not deserve what happened to me when I was a child. My power now, in how I let that affect the rest of my life.

My awareness prompted me to begin healing. The most difficult part was to forgive myself- for all the times I had played small or not set loving boundaries to protect myself as an adult. I naturally had loving compassion and empathy for others; I now began placing it upon myself.

Ultimately, I was now able to live more consciously and to recognise when I felt triggered. Utilising the various coping mechanisms above made it easier to move through the pain, to a place of peace, love and stillness.

"Change is inevitable but transformation is by conscious choice" -Heather Ash Amara

Choices are statements about your priorities and they indicate what you value. The natural progression from gaining awareness is living more consciously. Before, I didn't stop to consider how my choices in life were affecting its outcome, and often put the blame onto others when things fell apart. I now took responsibility for my life and how it had turned out. There was a sense of safety in living this way, but it was keeping me stuck. It also caused a lot of physical ailments, including depression and anxiety. It led me to engage in numbing behaviours, that were affecting my personal life, which further affected my mental health. It was a vicious circle.

The choices I was making did not reflect my true values. I was living in a way that was causing me inner turmoil and anguish. In doing the healing and becoming more aware, I was able to offer compassion to myself and to start making more conscious choices.

In society, there is an emphasis on putting others first, or risk being seen as being selfish. In making more conscious choices, I began to see things differently. It made me realise my happiness was important too. This desire to make others happy has been the most difficult habit to break. It is reinforced by deep abandonment wounds from my past. I wanted people to like and approve of me. However, in doing this, I was forgetting about if I actually liked and approved of myself.

I learned that I do have a choice and I can use my inner wisdom and intuition to help me make those choices. Some days it's easier to do than others, but instead of judging myself on these days, I find ways of nourishing myself. This often includes the choice not to do anything at all but rest and reflect. I also make a conscious choice to connect with my body through dance and meditation, which has shown me where I hold tension and stress. It alerts me to where I am not living in line with my authentic self.

One of the biggest conscious choices I made was to come off my antidepressants, after nearly a decade on them. This was done under the guidance of a doctor and various holistic therapists. I was unprepared for the level of repressed feeling that would resurface at this time. However, I trusted it was right for me, and I reached out to others to support me through this whole process. I found conscious dancing and women's retreats particularly helpful at this time. I learned to notice what feelings and sensations were coming up for me; through listening to the music and moving my body however it decided to move.

I was able to utilise those coping mechanisms previously mentioned, to hold me at my most vulnerable times. I made a conscious choice to not let fear hold me back and to connect with those feelings I had suppressed for so long. Making more conscious choices meant I was living more abundantly, and it was a catalyst for great change that benefited my authentic self immensely. Instead of seeing my anxiety as a problem, I took it as a warning sign that my choices were not in line with my higher self. I then took the steps to self-reflect and make more conscious ones.

Making more conscious choices filled me with a new zest for life. It spurred me on to make new connections and try new things. I was able to meet more like-minded people and built up a community that was able to support one and other on this journey.

"When you make a choice, you change the future" -Deepak Chopra

I am now able to live life making more conscious choices, which has led to great changes in my outlook, mental health and environment. Being able to sit with myself and tune into what I need has built up a level of trust and safety within me that has softened me. My heart is open to receiving and giving love freely, without conditions. It has made me want to protect myself from harsh energies and environments, and alerted me to what boundaries look like for me.

I now believe my time and energy are special. I want to be around people who genuinely care about me and are able to connect with me on a deeper level. Making the choice to remove toxic friends and family from my life was one of the most loving things I have done for myself. This was not an easy process as the feelings of guilt and shame arose. Sending out compassion to those whom I choose not to be around does help, and I can choose to love them from a distance. It has also created space in my life for more fulfilling relationships.

Somewhere I have always struggled was in romantic relationships. This is where my trauma and triggers reared their heads. I have learned so much about myself with each and every relationship, and am in a place now where I have chosen a partner much more consciously. I am open to learning, healing and growing, more than ever before. I see all relationships as a place to see the unhealed parts of me, and it offers an opportunity to bring them into the light, to be transformed.

I try to lead with my heart as opposed to my head. I chose to celebrate my femininity more and feel proud of being a woman. The magic and power we hold is phenomenal! I create space to carry out my own rituals/ceremonies, which often coincide with the moon cycles and the wheel of the year. This gives me the space to 'just be' and to reflect on my needs. I really believe in the power of intention and I lean into my own intuition. I treat myself with respect and love as much as I can.

Another key component in my transition to a more conscious life was in being able to both notice and soothe my nervous system when it became dysregulated. This would happen in times of stress, anxiety, frustration and relationship conflicts. Using this awareness, I am able to use different strategies to calm and soothe myself. These often include deep breathing, journaling, holding myself, wrapping myself up in a blanket, moving my body through dance or exercise and listening to music. Once I was regulated, I could become a loving parent to the scared little girl inside of me, and provide her with the reassurance that she is safe, divinely guided and protected.

I do not profess to know it all or have all the answers. Living more consciously is not an easy road and sometimes can be very lonely. However, in the end, it has led to deeper connections with people on a more authentic level. Ultimately, I try to take each day as it comes and live in the present moment. However, I am human and sometimes I do slip back into old stories. Yet I do not punish myself anymore. I acknowledge and accept it and I take the steps needed to get back on track. Life is a journey and not a destination. If we happen to meet upon the road, we can take each other's hands and guide each other through it.

Lorraine Ferguson, sand play therapist, trainee counsellor (student member of the BACP), and mother of one, who enjoys time in nature. Originally from Ireland but have lived in beautiful Derbyshire for 20 years now.

You can reach her at francesmorris8102@gmail.com

My Crone Song
Dawn Melling

I am Water, falling as torrents or tears
I am Earth, my pathways worn smooth by the years,
My voice is Air, rising like a hurricane set free
Then stilling soft and gentle - the exhale as I breathe.

Fire is my burning rage screaming in the night,
Turning soft as candle flames so Death may have a light.
I am the cat who waits, silent as a stone,
Patient as a carved sphinx, a talisman of bone.

I am Spirit, blessed and cursed, not knowing which is what,
The knower and the knowing, the stirrer of the pot,
All complete, the spell is spun,
I'm where I ended but just begun.

- Starlight Dawn

Learning to Align
Lucy Ascham

Fear is a physical set of sensations. Breath stopped. Eyes wide in horror. Mouth open in disbelief. Breath in through mouth. Tummy clenched. Brain whirring trying to make sense. Frozen to the spot. Trying to figure out the next move. Fear can give us a space to figure out our best route to safety – freeze, run, fight or faun. I know this and have been working on consciously releasing the fear response in my brain and body for years with myself and clients.

We had walked through the allotments, past the duck pond and the woods. We were home. I put my key in the lock, and looked down at my son's twinkling eyes. He had fun and anticipation on his face.

I turned the key but it didn't work. I tried again - confusion flooding my brain. Why isn't it working? What could it be? And why was my 3-year-old giggling?

"Daddy's played a trick!"

He knew something...

What? What…?!!

I went cold, and hot, and felt sick. A wave of incomprehension washed though my brain. My body, numb.

Shock!

My key didn't work.

I was locked out of my own house!

The next steps were small and basic. Call on a neighbour to use their bathroom. Try not to show my distress to my son. Waiting and waiting for him to come home and explain. My brain trying, and failing to make sense!

And then, my ex-partner appeared – smiling – and talking to our son. I explained my key hadn't worked. "Yes" he said. He had changed the locks. He picked up our son, walked into the house and shut the door.

My son's dad had changed the locks on me, without warning, communication or consent.

I had been locked out of my own house. I stood there shaking. Crying. Frozen. Winded.

Fear is a physical set of sensations. Breathing stopped. Eyes wide in horror. Mouth open in disbelief. Breath in through mouth. Tummy clenched.

Brain whirring trying to make sense. Frozen to the spot. Trying to figure out my next move.

I went to a neighbour's house and sat and cried. I tried to phone, but he didn't pick up. I went back to the flat where I'd been staying and one step after another, slowly, slowly, started to exist in this new foreign reality.

Over time, I've realized how much pain that he was in too. This was the best move he could make to protect his heart. He speaks with actions, not words or negotiations. I don't blame him. And I can be angry about his actions, which have had a huge impact on me, even after many years.

I know we were both hurting; our relationship was on the rocks. We were both scared. Both vulnerable. Both doing the best we could. He also had more power than me, more resources, and this moment made that super clear. In this world, it is often the man who has the upper hand financially and therefore a greater range of choices and comfort.

At the time, this moment felt like a huge granite mountain had stepped on me, like a small grey pebble, squashed into soft mud. I sank and gave way. I was overcome. I spent many months water-logged, crying, wondering why? why me? why did it have to end like this?

Over the years, I have come out of the squashed hole. I've got solid ground under my feet. I've regained my full human size, bit by bit. Now he is a man. No longer looming over me the whole time, and my every waking thought – he is just a man. Nowadays, I experience him more like an irritating stone in my shoe.

My story begins several months before my key didn't work. I'd been staying in a nearby apartment to rest and get clear about the warning signs my body was giving me. Life looked good. I lived in a beautiful house across the road from a duck pond and wooded valley, near some allotments. I lived with my mate, my partner, my lover- my son's father. I had relatively good health, enough money to buy new clothes in John Lewis and shop at Waitrose. My son was 2-years-old and the apple of my eye. I had made some friends since moving to Sheffield, when I was heavily pregnant, and enjoyed the daily activities, meet ups and play dates.

And yet, I was miserable…

All the outer signs promised a good life. But I was lonely, unconfident and unsatisfied. I was also scared. On my birthday I always got a big bunch of lilies from my partner. I accidentally knocked them over when putting my son down, and I went into panic. Some of the pollen had gone on his cream sofa!! I stopped breathing. I phoned the cleaning specialists and tried to find out what to use to clean this spot. I was too scared to tell my partner.

Oh wait! No, that's not a good sign. When he saw the stain later and I told him what happened, he didn't say a word. He didn't look at me. He went and got a cloth, some product and sat and dabbed at it for an hour. No words. No eye contact.

I felt crushed.

As human beings, we need to know we matter. To know we exist. I wanted him to know my intentions were good, and to relate. I depended on this man for so much; even down to knowing if I even existed or not!

This was far from the only occasion when I have been shocked and frightened about what was happening in my world.

The thing I began to realise is that this pattern of 'not-talking about difficult things' didn't begin with him, or me. My parents would sometimes 'have moments' of conflict about money. My dad bought a fancy new HiFi and mum worried about feeding and clothing us 5 kids. I didn't understand the conversations, which seemed to be based on the fact money had been spent on a luxury without mutual agreement, and my mum had to make the rest of the budget stretch for food and clothing. Honestly, as the youngest of 5 I can't tell you how many patches I had on the hand-me-downs from siblings and jumble sales.

I was used to this dynamic: the man seems devoted and looks after himself and his needs, and yes also does practical things for the family. But the undercurrents were strong and I could feel moments of being dragged by the undertow. As a little girl I didn't understand the words, but I could read the energy of a situation well. I learned how to keep small, to stay safe. I don't mean to judge my parents- more to say that I grew up with this pattern, so my soul recognised it so strongly when I met my son's father. Consciously, I would not have chosen to repeat this pattern; subconsciously, I recognised it and chose it.

I became a woman making do, putting a smile on my face and keeping the show on the road. This time, I had John Lewis clothes and food from Waitrose so I didn't realise I had been repeating this family pattern. It all felt normal because it was so familiar to my childhood. I couldn't recognise the pattern because it felt like home.

Yes, there were some red flag moments, but the needs that were met far outweighed the difficulties and challenges initially. I have many communication skills and hope that I would manage better and find ways for all of us to thrive.

The awareness around the bigger picture came when I took space for myself. To slow down. To cut out the noise and busyness. To feel my body just lying on the floor, looking at the ceiling and the sky. Nothing to do. Nothing to get right. No one else to be responsible for half an hour at a time. I had been practicing this art of resting for 10 years or more. It's also known as Constructive Rest in the Alexander Technique.

Despite my best efforts, I had been subsumed by moving to a new city, a tricky pregnancy, birth trauma, motherhood and so many sleepless nights. After the sad realization that I was no longer welcome in my own house, the floor felt like the safest place. I couldn't fall off the floor. This was surely as low as I could go.

So, I would use lying-on-the-floor-time, to slowly come awake and aware again. These quiet moments of me, my breath, my body and the floor were life changing. This spaciousness helped me begin to know what I wanted, what I needed, what mattered. That *I mattered*.

Taking space to really slow down and listen to myself also helped me begin to realise what I didn't want, what didn't suit me, what hurt, what confused me, what troubled me and what I didn't want to put up with anymore. These quiet times helped me feel supported by the ground. Helped me to reconnect with my body – just me. Not me and baby – *ME* again. I reconnected my thoughts to the current moment. To the simple moments; and found I could once again talk kindly to my body and create the best conditions inside me to unfurl, to decompress, to cry, to reclaim my full size.

I know how to rest consciously and constructively – this is something I now share in my work.

I had very few of my things so the choices were slim. I was in a beautiful flat near some woods and when I felt the urge I would go and walk.

I began to befriend myself, to know myself, to nurture myself.

The biggest shift now was childcare. I was the stay-at-home mum, by choice and privilege. But now, my son was with his dad or his nanny and I was alone for many more hours and days than I wanted or knew what to do with.

This was hard. Hard to accept. Hard to live with, as it was NOT what I wanted. My heart felt crushed.

Every week, at this point, I had a call to America with Sarah Peyton, who gave me empathy. All my thoughts and feelings were held with such care and warmth. She kept track of me and my life; never or super rarely, offering advice - and always asking for consent first. This part is so important. Advice is mostly unhelpful when repairing from trauma.

Consistent accompaniment was what I needed. Someone to see how precarious life was for me internally. How sweet, when someone understood how shocked, wounded and bewildered I was!

Sarah saw me just as I was; tearful, snotty, shocked, and I could tell her anything. She was so consistent in 'being there for me, and with me'. I was not broken. She didn't try and fix me. And gradually, I healed. My brain rewired from trauma and became a kinder place to be.

In my fear and alarmed aloneness, she kept seeing me, helping me feel my feelings and made it possible to time travel in my mind. To accompany me in the scariest, earlier moments and safely help me unfreeze and bring the younger me back to my heart, back to now. I sobbed and raged, wilted and withered. With her care, over time, I stopped waking every night, replaying conversations I wish I'd had and making bargains with The Judge who'd ordered a 50:50 child-care arrangement. Gradually, I slept better when my boy was away. Gradually I learned to say 'Yes' to my new reality. My life as an Alexander Technique teacher is all about conscious choice. I really value this as a somatic experience- an embodied reality. I love consideration and communication - if I were a piece of Blackpool rock I would have 'connection' written inside me.

Sadly, I was unable to make deals with my ex which felt good for me. I was unable to negotiate, as it seemed I was the only one willing to shift. Sporadic emails only listed my failings and wrongness and didn't fit with 'his agreement', whatever that means. I learned to keep quiet, not to ask, not to reach out. One step forward, two back.

But that unique spark of me and my life would not stay lying down.

My mothering instincts and love made me fierce. My need for justice kept me asking for what I thought was best for our child. Less time with the Nanny and more with his Mummy.

I was reading books about women who had been snatched off the street and held hostage for years. I read books about people walking on their own as pilgrims, with no money for a year. I read a book about how Victor Frankl survived concentration camps. Knowing we can't always choose our circumstances, but we can choose our responses to life, in mind, body and lived reality. Reading helped me see my story in other people's lives and see how they had experienced far more horrific things and survived. This gave me hope and courage and a shared reality.

In my own way, I became more courageous and creative. I sought help from counsellors, play therapists, friends, family, colleagues, nonviolent communication coaches and solicitors. I learned how to stand up for my needs and my son's wellbeing. Time and time again. Did I get what I wanted because I could ask more kindly? Absolutely not. What I did learn was to be on my own side. To know what I valued and to keep asking. To keep showing up for my needs, my son's wellbeing and my vision of what could be better.

I don't have to like the answers I get (or no answer at all). I'm not a 'bad person' or 'selfish' if I take care of myself. I am responsible for myself, and cannot give from an empty cup. I recognize I can't please everyone all the time - and it's not my job to do so. Family Constellations has been a huge part of my healing process. And now I'm trained as a facilitator, I am able to offer others a new lens with which to see their life. I love to help others connect with hidden resources and find strength in their roots, within their family system.

When we are in the midst of pain, we sometimes only see the details and lose the bigger picture. Constellations can offer the widest, deepest view on life experiences and help bring movement to seemingly stuck situations. It is my favourite way to help rewire my brain and nervous system by transforming my perception.

My heart has grown bigger over the years. My perspective on these painful moments has become wider, I'm learning to include everyone and everything in my heart.

Of course, I still have strong preferences, and I have access to more of my emotions when things don't go as I'd like. I also have more scope for acceptance when I don't get what I want or need, and learning to live well with that. Not as a martyr, but with mourning for my lost hopes and dreams, and a softening in my heart and body which comes with that. I have more peace in my heart, in spite of and because of my experiences, choices and fate.

One thing I know for sure, there are some greater forces at play in my life. I aim to navigate life with recognition of the unseen undercurrents, how they push and pull me in life, and to learn to accept these with love. I bow to my fate. And accept my Life at this cost.

As a Constellations Facilitator, it's like being the captain of a ship for others too. To go out to sea and explore their depths, their pain and deep longings, and bring them back safely to port. Changed by their voyage and new views, ready for their next step; with more resources, more love and their ancestors' blessings as they move forwards.

All the scary moments I have had, led to me becoming stronger and softer. Wiser, and aware how little I know. More self-full and more generous. My heart is bigger because of all it can encompass. Neither right nor wrong. Being full of compassion and being on everyone's side - that's my aim.

Saying 'Yes' to reality. So that we can let our energy, our life-energy flow forwards into our life, with the blessings of our ancestors - for us to have an easier time than they did.

If I had to, I would do it all again – for the love of my son.

I'm good now. I have my own home, my Loving Nest.

I know more about who I am, what I had already suffered in my childhood, which meant I recognized the odd shapes I took to fit in with my ex. I recognised him and his misshapen heart too. We tried; I know I tried all I knew, to fit into that life together. The cost of staying was too high. I needed to know I belonged, that I mattered, that I existed! These were my heart and soul wounds which came to light in this relationship, and are healing.

I can see this pain-pattern more clearly and where it's come from, in him and me. Our families were both affected directly and indirectly by WWII, rationing, surviving. Somewhere, on a soul level - our wounds matched. His and mine- in size and weight. That is how we recognised each other. That was part of the attraction. Part of the cost of loving each other.

I'm sure our souls still love each other. Our energies came together, as they had to, to bring forth our beautiful boy.

And yet, sadly, as humans we couldn't figure out how to make the relationship work.

Resonant Language with Sarah Peyton has been a huge part of my healing journey. Sarah meets me where I am -with constant curiosity. Her gaze and warmth holding me, my body sensations, emotions with exquisite compassion. The brain can be healed from trauma; we can rewire our brain and make it a happier place to live.

I'm now in training to learn how to do this for others. Sessions are available.

Other people who know and love me think they'd have known better or seen the troubles ahead. I don't know if they really did. I don't know if I'd have done anything differently even if that were true. I was in love. I have learned so much about little Lucy, the traumas she felt and how much holding and healing she needed. And how different I am now. Calmer, angrier, kinder, wiser, more humble, fiercer, more rounded and resourced- and ready to help.

If after reading this you think I can help, please get in touch. I work in person and online with individuals and groups in Sheffield, and worldwide on Zoom. Helping to resolve and integrate pain in the body, emotions, and soul.

lucy@lucyascham.com

www.lucyascham.com

I'm Possible
Judith Quin

It's impossible to believe
It's impossible to conceive
It's impossible to see
When you're lost in the dark.

It's impossible to know
It's impossible to show
It's impossible to grow
When you think others must be right
And you have learned to diminish your light.

It's impossible to shine
It's impossible to be ...
Whoever or whatever you're really supposed to be
If you can't see
Beyond the bounds of what others say is true
It's impossible to really be you.

But

There in the dark is the seed
Of the you that exists in full flight
All you need is a chink of light
And when the conditions are right
You just might ...

Feel like your world is crumbling down, falling apart,
Breaking open wide.
Don't lose heart.

When the cracks appear, the light is near
So let your chinks open wide.
Step out of the night, let in the light,
And you just might start to see..

That it is possible to believe
It is possible to conceive
Everything you have dreamed in to being.

So say it with me:
"I'm Possible."

It is possible to know
It is possible to grow
It is possible to show the way.

So say it with me now:
"I'm Possible."

It is possible to shine
And as you start your climb
It is possible to light the way
For others who are still stuck in their dark.

So say it like you mean it:
"I'm Possible!"

Say it like you think it could be true
Like you believe there is something more
In this world for you.

Say it like you mean it
Like there's something in your heart
That needs to be heard
And it's YOU.

"I'm Possible."

Say it every day
And even when it's dark
You'll find that light again
Because the source of that light lives in you.

And when you know that to be true…

You ARE Possible.

If people can fly in steel machines
If we can go to the moon
If diseases can be cured
And if you have survived all that you've endured….

What else might be possible too?

Judith Quin
Founder: Your Whole Voice
https://yourwholevoice.com
Instagram.com/yourwholevoice

Pain – Healing – Love

Lucy A Collins

Pain

Pain can mean many kinds of things. There are many different kinds of pain, you see. There is pain that will help you transform and there is pain that will help you see things in a different light. Nothing is sent to punish you. Your only job whilst on this earthly plane is to transform from one iteration to the next. By that, I mean to a newer and wiser version of you. There is nothing on this planet that was sent to 'destroy' you, as so many of you say. Nothing can be destroyed in any case as. After all kinds of pain, you still exist. You survived it. You are here, therefore you cannot be destroyed. Ever. You see, child, there are many different ways you can see pain too. The pain that is deep in your heart is a calling to return back to you; to go beyond this pain and find out who you really are. For you are not pain, and you are not any of the things that happened to you. You are blessed with the light of abundance- an abundance that is infinite. An abundance of light and joy which is far, far greater than any pain you might experience and is all you need to transform into something greater. In this respect, you are like a butterfly, my child. A butterfly endures extreme pain, as it emerges from its chrysalis. And how does it emerge afterwards? In the most beauteous splendour, and that is how I intended it to be.

Your life is not about pain and was never intended to be about pain. Can you go beyond the pain and see how it was meant to transform you? Can you see how you were not meant to endure the pain- but also become the beauteous, majestic butterfly who emerged in spite of all that happened? It burned through all of the pain and emerged beauteous, majestic and splendid. And that is what I want for you, butterfly. That is what you came here to do – to emerge from your pain and flourish – that was your only job here. So, whenever you feel alone in your pain, remember that you are so gently and lovingly held. No matter how dark things seem, you are always held and you are never alone. You can never be alone, you just have little understanding of what walks besides you, what loves you and what holds you, no matter what. Those tears you cry are rivers of healing, so let them wash away the pain and let them heal. You came here to be free and the way to freedom is right through your pain.

Face it, head-on, and allow it to do its divine work so that you can do yours.

You are here to be splendid like the butterfly, and, once you have burned through the pain, you will barely remember who you were before. Do you think that the butterfly spends much time thinking about the caterpillar that it was before? No, the butterfly is far too busy being supported by its own wings that were formed by the burning and the pain. So, find your wings, that's your only job. Find your wings and fly. And remember that you are loved and you cannot fail. Find your wings and jump! Jump, you say? But I'm scared. Scared is nothing to be afraid of. Scared when you are jumping means that you are ready, that's all. 'Ready' means jumping scared. Remember that you cannot fail, and we will always be here to help you, just remember to ask. Remember the times when we asked you to jump and you wouldn't jump? That was just fear talking louder than love- but you are loved, and love is always greater than fear. Your fear will disappear when you jump into love, but you need to be brave enough to jump through the fire. No-one else can do it for you. We can only coax you with challenges, but you have to be the one who jumps- who trusts and then jumps. We will catch you, of course, but you have to jump. So, jump. Jump! Jumping is the only way you can save yourself. Did you really think that I would allow someone to come and save you or, indeed, that I would come and save you? My dear, that's simply not the done-thing when you know that you are such a splendid being of light, capable of all things- and especially of saving yourself. This isn't just about you; this is about all of us. In saving yourself, you teach others how to do the same. Raise the vibration and shed light on the path, so that others can use it to move forwards and shine, just like you did and you can. I know you can.

You have it in you because you are me.

Healing

What is healing, if not to pour light into open wounds and cleanse and close with love? What does it mean to heal? Exactly as I said. Look for the light and allow it to fill up all wounds. Wounds are there to teach you what you came here to do, and point you in the direction of your greatest wisdom. Healing is a truly wondrous thing you can do for yourself. But how do you heal, you say? How? As if to pain yourself with the question of how? Or, but whyyy?! Healing can never be found there, in those kinds of questions. For healing, we must look elsewhere and find a reason to overcome the darkness. The darkness is there to help you find the light- the light within, that shines so brightly, but has been dimmed with all these woundings. Well, what I say is that the woundings can be cleansed away. Think of them as smudges on a wondrously bright lantern and its shine has been dulled somewhat by layers of dust. But the light beneath still shines so brightly and perfect as it ever has, like when it first came into existence. Its light can never be extinguished by something as inconsequential as a layer of dust. Do you see where we're going here? You are perfect and whole as you are, in this body- this body of light; and all you have to do is remove what is covering it. Do you remember how we said that pain hasn't been sent to punish you? Well, it hasn't. It never was. There are merely a set of lessons designed for the advancement of your soul. The more you take these in hand and really seek to uncover the brilliance underneath, the more you will see that none of this was sent to harm you. You can never be fully harmed, because your light will always shine, no matter what. That light that is hidden is truly brilliant- know that it's the thing that makes you truly you, and truly unique. It's that special. So, you see, this whole thing we have with identifying with our pain is a distraction from the true work of what you came here to do- and that is to shine brilliantly and unapologetically. Forget what happened in the past. What past? All that matters is that you are here, now, in this moment, and that you are safe in this moment. That's all you need to do to return to you – just return to this moment and *know* that you are ok.

Healing just means taking all of the pain and transforming it into light. Light is where creation begins. From light, you can begin to create something truly beautiful from the ashes of everything that burned-like the butterfly emerging. This is how you do it. This is how you become free of the past. This is how you are in the eternal sunshine of this beingness that you are radiating on earth. There is a power in your shine once it has been fully released, especially after it has taken much time to uncover it. There is hope for all, and if you can just cling to that hope and expand it into true believing then, my child, the world is yours. I know you have much to say, yet you are covering up the brilliance of your contribution to humanity-through your commitment to honouring your pain and re-living it. There is a certain kind of loyalty to pain, as if you can be nothing beyond this; but it doesn't serve you to choose this path and it certainly doesn't serve anyone else. Remember who you are. You are not pain and you are not suffering. This is the game – to remember who you truly are and show up in the full knowledge of the remembering, that you came here to shine. There is much love- more love than you can ever imagine- on the other side of fear, and everything else that you believe is preventing you from embracing the fullness of who you really are. I remember. I know. It's time that you remember and you know. There is so much to be gained from taking life by the reins, letting it guide you through the tumultuousness and allowing life to be your anchor at those times of darkness. Remember that darkness is sent to serve you and to remind you to move forwards, and that this darkness is not who you are. You are light, remember? You are light. It's time to shine and let us know who you really are.

All you need to remember is that you are loved without measure.

Love

What can I say about love, other than I love you? Love is all there is and all there ever was. What does it mean to be in love? What is the meaning of love? To love means to love yourself deeply; to dive into the magnificence of all that is love. Love is meant to motivate you to become who you were meant to be. Be motivated by love instead of fear. Choose the loving option, and that means choosing the most loving option for yourself. This means choosing for you alone, no matter what the external circumstances are telling you. Coming from a place of love means embracing all the love that exists in the now, because in the here and now, you are loved and you are safe.

To love is to be adored by your own self; to love so deeply as if no other option exists, which it doesn't. Your only true option is to embrace love and also the uncertainty that comes with love. Only fear has all the answers, and fear will tell you that it certainly knows the answers. And fear will tell you that it certainly knows the way in all the detail. Fear truly 'knows' what will happen- except fear really knows nothing at all, other than what it thinks it knows from past experiences. But past experiences tell you nothing of your full potential. Fear is there to signpost what it knows, based on learned experiences. But what it 'learned' can be very shaky anyway, as it came from a very limited perspective of the tiny dot of the whole that it saw. There is another perspective, and I say that you are not your fear. That fear isn't even really yours, it's just a construct that was necessary at the time but it isn't anymore. Return to the love, embrace love, and see what that will do for you instead. If you have so many results in life already from embracing fear (and those results have been spectacularly successful based on the place you created them from), what would happen if you fully chose love instead, and fully made decisions from a place of true, true love instead? Of true, true love for yourself above all else? Do you know what will happen if you do that? Stupendously magnificent results that you will love. How about that?

What if I told you that you cannot fail? As long as you are breathing and alive, you are winning. There is no such thing as failure whilst there is still a game to play and we are playing for love now, remember? There is only one way out and that way is through love. The thing is, it may not seem as love at first. The key here is discernment. Can you check in with yourself enough to know when something is coming from love or fear? Can you fully *know* that? That's where the treasure lies. You don't need to know this the way that the mind knows things. That is something else entirely. Our old friend, the mind, operates according to its own rules and is part of the game. Mind is there to check: "Are you choosing for you? Are you *fully* choosing for you? Can you fully go beyond fear and choose love anyway?"

The key to life is this: Are you happy? Are you joyous? Are you fully choosing the things that bring you joy? There isn't really anything to it other than that. Ah, but the past, you say? And I say but what about the past? What does that have to do with you or any of your magnificent self? The past is just part of the puzzle- part of the game, and it's up to you to decide how you will use it. That's the game here – you have infinite power, over yourself and your decisions. Can you fully step into that power, own your decisions and fully step into making decisions from a place of abundant love? Heal not your sorrow, but drink in your joy and let it runneth over. Does that scare you? Good. Now we have something real we can work with. Why are you so afraid of living in your joy? What are all those fears that just ambushed your mind? And are you ready to overcome them and choose joy anyway? Are you ready to jump into joy and embrace all that joy has to offer- because *that* is true love right there. Can you be your own true love? That's the only thing that matters. That's the game right there. And if you remember only one thing from this, remember that you were truly loved all along. The rest is on you.

Can you love yourself as deeply as I am asking?

Lucy A Collins describes herself as an explorer and an adventurer, who has already made it to around 55 countries and counting! It was a deep sense of curiosity and wonder, plus a love of personal growth and development that led Lucy to discover that she had an unusual talent for receiving answers to profound questions, which is the inspiration behind Pain – Healing – Love.

In her professional life, Lucy is a writing services virtual assistant based in Nottingham, UK who helps heart-led leaders find the words to express their brilliance. Lucy works with solopreneurs, life coaches and business owners who want to show up, shine and make a positive impact in the world. Lucy loves this because she gets to make the world a better place one client at a time.

You can contact Lucy at inspiredwritingbylucy@gmail.com.

Love is the Answer
Maria Atherley

It's most common for me to gain sparks of Divine Inspiration from song. As someone who works with sound and frequency for a living now, this feels fitting and almost the 'least spooky' way of getting 'downloads' and 'messages'.

When I tune in to the frequency of fear, this is what comes through:

> *"You turn around and life's passed you by*
> *You look to ones you love to ask them why*
> *You look to those you love to justify*
> *You turned around and life's passed you by*
> *Passed you by again."*
> *- Doves – There Goes the Fear*

This journey of healing, and ultimately connecting with our divinity, for me is eloquently summarised in the chorus of this 2002 Indie anthem.

Ultimately, I believe the biggest fear we all have is that of a life half-lived. Of regret for not taking the risk to jump, have the difficult conversation, make the heartfelt apology before it's too late. That we will go to our earthly graves not realising that we could or should have made that decision, taken the leap of faith, been brave enough. Fear sits inside each and every one of us and will eat away at us, if we allow it.

So, for those of us brave souls embarking on this journey of healing – all we are doing is facing this fear and finding our sacred 'No'.

Saying that I will no longer be content to live half a life.

That I will not be sated or satisfied from looking back and having regrets.

That mediocrity and mundanity are not enough to say I lived a full and magical life on this earth plane!

Once this fear is faced and stared back at, when you look yourself in the eye and make a commitment to act – this is when the magic really begins to show itself.

When I look back – the signs were there all along. The deeper I have gone on my forward journey and the lighter I have become in my frequency, the more I have been able to see the breadcrumb trails left for me by the Divine... As if they were waiting for me to wake up!

All my life, I have been in and of service to others. I began my 'career' in hospitality, transitioning to Human Resources and now as a Sound Healer and Ceremonial Space Holder.

Music and sound have always played a big part in my life. As a young girl my bedroom walls were plastered with posters of my favourite bands. I learned to play the recorder and flute through school. I studied music to A Level. As a university student, I found my love for live music- which continues to this day. Even my son is a gifted guitar and bass player now. The fact that the mantra chanting part of kundalini yoga hooked me in to the Naad energy, 'the cosmic sound', shouldn't really have come as no surprise to me!

When I attended my first sound bath in 2017, I knew there was so much 'technology' in this healing – it took me to even deeper places than I had already experienced. Once I really started working with instruments like gongs, singing bowls and tuning forks, I knew this was the present and future of healing. I feel so very blessed to have made these (re)connections.

Throughout my life (this time!), I have never stopped learning. I have always been curious to know, experience, see and be more. I was somewhat of a diligent student at school and university, then as an adult, I have had a consistent desire to grow and continue learning. I don't ever see this changing. The future of humanity and all our potentiality excites me so much!

The relationship between me and my earthly body has also been an interesting one. Through my healing journey and the many embodied practices and methodologies I have experienced- over the last six years in particular - I can now say that I love and respect my body. I used to be disconnected from it – dislike, even hate parts of it! Now, through the work I have done to reconnect the 'dismembered' parts of myself – childhood woundings, parental imprints, generational trauma, birth trauma, issues with my menarche and adolescence and more recently, deep womb healing- I have come to know and love all aspects of ME. And in doing this, I have expanded and grown in ways I could never have imagined.

How this plays out in the day to day living of a human life is the most interesting and important part.

I feel like I am fearless now – like absolutely nothing can faze me.

So, this is me in 2022. Nearly 6 years in to my catalogued and deliberately orchestrated 'Awakening'. But in actual reality, it has been evolving in me since I incarnated under a Capricorn Sun and a Virgo Moon, way, way, back in December 1972.

Flashing backwards to October 2016, I found myself committing the last £1000 of my divorce money to take myself away on a 'Mind, Body and Soul Retreat' to Ibiza. This retreat was organised by the gym I was then a member of – I was going away for a re-set. It felt significant. I was leaving my partner, son and two stepchildren for a week, to 'indulge' myself. Oh - how I underestimated what I would experience!!

The setting was rustic, peaceful and idyllic. Balearic autumnal sun and very chilled vibes. A group of familiar strangers, thrown together to eat well, train hard and do some 'inner work'. On the itinerary was Sunrise Yoga with Nina. I think I may have been the only one in the group who did an excited little squeal! I am an early bird and have practiced yoga on and off since the late 1990's – not the most committed student, but not entirely a novice either. I was really looking forward to this. I seem to recall that Nina had explained to us that we would be working through the 'chakras' – energy centres located around the body, to systematically unlock and smooth out any imbalances. Her style of teaching was different. She had a fierce and loving authority. I felt safe. She commanded the group with her firm but gentle voice. She sang and chanted. She played beautiful music and chimes. I was all in.

By Day 3, we were working on the solar plexus. I cannot even recall now what it was we were doing. All I know now is, what happened next was the real beginning of my embodied awakening in the physical. Through a combination of breathwork, movement and chanting, I found myself in a state of uncontrollable release. Sobs racked my body and tears flowed like rivers. I could not stop. Some of the other students motioned to comfort me, but Nina held them back.

"Let her cry – it's fine", she said.

And cry I did. For hours and hours. Like a small child in the night, waking from a nightmare and sobbing inconsolably. I was exhausted. Unable to participate in whatever activities were scheduled for the rest of that morning. We ventured out as a group in the afternoon for a walk to Es Vedra – said to be one of the most magnetic points on the planet and a site of spiritual pilgrimage for many. I walked and cried simultaneously. Each footfall releasing more pain into the earth. As a group we laid stones in a labyrinth. I was able to say goodbye finally!

What left my body that day was 4 years' worth of grief, pain and life trauma. Lodged right in my solar plexus. In Sanskrit the solar plexus is called *Manipura* – 'the Lustrous Gem'. Interestingly, it's where we hold our sense of personal joy and willpower. It is also where our power becomes eroded if we hang on to feelings of sadness and disempowerment.

From this moment on – Tuesday 18th October 2016, I was a different person. Something inside of me had changed irrevocably. From that experience I had been able to truly feel what it was like to begin healing a part of me that was broken and lost – disconnected from me, yet still part of me.

In December 2012 my beautiful sister-in-law Cassie, passed away suddenly, yet peacefully in her sleep, aged 36. What followed was the (inevitable) ending of my 21-year long relationship with her brother, only 6 months after her death. I became a 'single mum', aged 40. I knuckled down to the job in hand, navigating through the tides of change which ensued – house moves, keeping my job, handling time away from my then 9-year-old son and dealing with the new relationship dynamic with my ex-husband. Time passed and I met someone special. He just happened to be married, with two young children. Our relationship deepened and he chose a new life with me. We set up home together in 2015. By the end of that year, I had left full-time employment to pursue building my own HR consultancy. Things felt like they were in flow.

But all of this time, I had not really allowed myself to properly grieve for my sister, who I had known for

20 years when she passed. Or release the loss of my 21-year relationship, and all that had led to its breakdown. Or process the guilt of being part of breaking up the family home of my now second husband. Or release the fear of stepping out of the safety of a well-paid, 'safe' career into the unknown blackhole of self-employment. Upon reflection, I was holding on to a lot!

Through the embodied practice of kundalini yoga, I had begun the process of letting it all go.

On the flight back I made a commitment to continue a regular practice with this yoga. By December 2016 I had signed up for my first teacher training, qualifying as a Kundalini Yoga Teacher by February 2018.

The release I had back in Ibiza was a catalyst for self-initiated change. There was no doubt in any part of me that things would ever be the same again. The physicality of the practice was like nothing I had experienced previously. It dislodged something in me. Created space. And a level of deep enquiry that, at the time, I didn't appreciate where it was leading me towards.

Since 2017, life, and all of its wondrous mysteries has expanded, deepened, and become richer in ways I could never have imagined. My perspective has changed on many things; I question way more than I used to. I trust my intuition more and those in authority less. Having always been a 'good girl', this has taken a lot of unravelling! I listen to my body.

I have been held safely by my husband, who in all honesty has been my enabler. Having seen the profound changes in me, as well as my determination to evolve – he has very much been along for the ride and by my side. And of course, there have been benefits for him too. A more considered, caring and unconditionally loving wife, who is more present, patient and giving. I am forever grateful to him for allowing this transformation and more importantly, for resonating with my journey.

The last 6 years have taken me to some dark and painful places. I have cried, shouted, sobbed and been in a lot of physical pain at times. I don't necessarily expect this to change as time flows forwards either! Healing and the integration of that healing hurts. This work asks us to face aspects of ourselves and experiences in our lives that we have suppressed and hidden away. It's dirty and messy. And expansive, enabling and powerful – all at the same time!

And ultimately, to what end?

I feel now that I am at the beginning of the third iteration of my human beingness in this lifetime. As someone who is in service to humanity, for the purpose of healing, enlightenment and connecting as many people as possible with their true purpose as I can.

There are certain memories in my life that will remain imprinted in my heart forever. The day I got married to my first husband. The moment I touched my son and kissed him for the first time, after he was removed from my womb. The day I married my Beloved John. I could go on, as there are so many.

Snapshots in time from the beautiful camera of my mind, forever captured. Sometimes they are movies, sometimes they are photographs.

Until very recently I had not worked out what this meant and how significant they are to us.

But I know now.

With every fibre of my human being-ness, I know.

For certain.

A cog has turned on the wheel of conscious evolution in my mind, and it cannot go in any direction but forwards now.

I invite you now to try something for me, as you are reading these words...

Cast your mind back to a treasured memory. Something that really holds a deep space in your heart.

It may be a moment of observational beauty – a flower, the sky, a sunrise. The photograph of a loved one. A birthday celebration. A wedding. The smell of your favourite cake baking in the oven. Your favourite song – the one you can remember all the lyrics to. A special conversation you had with an amazing person. The remembrance of holding someone's hand and the imprint it left. The tastes, textures, and saliva-inducing memories of the best meal you ever ate.

Find it. The memory. Cast your line and hook it in.

Get clear and delve into the detail.

Invoke the senses around it.

Colour.

Texture.

Taste.

Smell.

Shape.

Form and feel.

Breathe it in to your heart. And out again.

Sit up straight.

Open your airways.

Lift your head.

Unclench your jaw.

Drop your shoulders.

Soften your face.

And breathe.

Now close your eyes for a moment. Take your eyes of this page, close them, and go inside.

Welcome back to this page and these written words.

You just connected with the frequency of Joy.

If you were not brave enough to go inside, I invite you to re-read up to this point and try again.

Really feel it.

The colour, the temperature, the shape, and form of it. Maybe it has a sound? Or a taste left on your lips? A sensation somewhere in your body... a tingling... a feeling of complete freedom.

A moment of Joy, lodged in your memory!

What a gift.

This is what we all can access.

This is where my 'Spiritual Awakening' has led me so far.... The embodiment of Joy! And I anticipate that there will be much, much more to come and I am SO EXCITED to experience it all.

My name is Maria and I live in Sheffield with my husband John, son Jasper, step-children Lily and Henry and our sausage dog Colin! We love music, eating yummy food and having fun together. I spend a lot of time outdoors, walking our beautiful landscape in and around the Peak District and further afield throughout Yorkshire. I travel frequently to Somerset to connect with the land around Glastonbury-Avalon. You can find me smiling most, behind my gongs and singing bowls and holding space for beautiful souls in circle and ceremony. Reach out and connect through my website www.mariaatherley.com or visit me @mariaatherleyraisingyourvibe on Instagram, https://www.facebook.com/mariaatherleysoundtherapy on Facebook.

A Letter From your Soul-self
Robyn Harris

Dearest One,

I wanted to reach out to you; to say that I've seen the challenges you've been facing and all that you've been doing to navigate through the sometimes-stormy seas. I've watched you question yourself, wondering whether you have what it takes, whether you're making the right choices and, at times, if you'll ever make it through to calmer waters. I know that at times you've felt disorientated, lost and alone- even losing sight of the wonder of who you *really* are and the amazing gifts that you bring.

So, I wanted to let you know that, in fact, you are not alone. I am here, right by your side, all along the way. When times feel hard, I'm there supporting you; when times feel good, I'm there celebrating with you; when you feel that you're the only one on this path, just look up and you'll see me there, cheering you on.

You might not be able to see me with your eyes, but you will know and recognise me from your heart. I'm there in the little things: the sun after the rain, the refreshing rain at the end of a long hot day, the smile of a child, the purr of a cat, the wag of a dog's tail, the breeze through the leaves on a tree, and gently caressing your skin; the phone call or email from a friend, the ocean, the sunrise and sunset, the moon and the stars.

In all of these things, I send my love to you. I long to fill you and surround you with this love, and for it to empower you and to connect you with all the wisdom and resources that you carry within you.

But sometimes, I see that things weigh you down and blind you to my love. And so, I'm writing to tell you directly how special, how precious you are to me! I created you – over many generations – carefully selecting the very particular aspects of being that went into forming such a wanted and treasured child. Both the things that you have labelled 'good' and the things that you, or others, have called 'unwanted' or 'undesirable'. To me, they are all just aspects of my beloved child. Both 'good' and 'undesirable' have their strengths and weaknesses, but when they come together in the love I wish to share with you, then their true beauty, power and majesty shine for all to see. Then love, light and joy shine from you, onto all around you - and light up the world with that love.

Please take these words to your heart, dear one. Release your worries and fears and your need to take life so seriously. Relax into the knowledge of my love and the safe space in which you are so gently held. Life is not a test. You can't get it 'wrong' or 'fail'. If things don't work out the way you'd hoped, just smile. Call out 'Plot twist!', and start over. I'll be right there, laughing along with you and cheering you every step of the way.

And if you ever need to feel my presence; to feel my arms around you and to know the truth of all that I've shared- just find a place of stillness, close your eyes and gently reach out with your heart. I'll be there.

Yours always, forever,
Your Soul-Self.

Robyn Harris, Equenergy: W·I·L·D Wellbeing
https://equenergy.com
https://equenergy.com/group

Creating a Future with Hope
Marie Batty

When I was close to breaking point, I could see exactly the direction life was heading in; for myself, and for my daughters. I could find no help with improving our health. I dreaded my work as a supply teacher and no longer believed all the energy I was putting in was making a difference.

I had absolutely no idea that I was on the brink of shifting, from a paradigm of fear, to cultivating a deep trust- in the perfect unfolding of the mystery of our divine paths.

For me, the biggest transformations have been the result of learning to reconnect, with myself and feel my feelings. Feelings are our precious communications; ever present, always here to help and guide us.

Through an awareness of our feelings and in choosing to surrender, we have an ability to blossom into our lives. To return to harmony and to allow all the blessings and love in the universe to flow in and through us. This energy, that we are all able to access, at any time, has the potential to improve our lives. To impact those around us and the whole planet!

Surrender gives us the ability to connect with a force that's greater than ourselves and unlock the potential of all that we are yet to understand.

In these essays I hope to explore the nature of feelings and share some of my own experiences on the power of surrender.

Fear

Since starting this journey of spiritual awakening, I have gained a new, kinder view of myself and others. I see now that I am more forgiving. I've moved into a better place in my life and I'm proud of the person I've become. These were never things I imagined I would say about myself.

For most of my life, it felt like the outcome was always destined to be disappointment. It felt like a lifetime of struggling with my health, my mental health and me messing things up.

With every new endeavour, I tried so hard- I would truly give it my all. But before long, the cracks would appear and then everything I'd tried so hard to achieve would come crumbling down around me. This was because I was always looking outside of myself for a better life. I thought a career, or money, or a relation-ship could make life better. Because they made me feel good, and everyone else seemed to want them too. I believed those things I was striving for would make everything ok. But, no matter how much effort I put in, things never seemed to work out.

My feelings about myself would descend, down, down, down.

Down to the belief that me being in the world is damaging, that it would be better for everyone if I wasn't here.

That by becoming a mother I've done the worst possible thing to the two people I love the most.

My daughters have been a huge part of my awakening journey- It was seeing patterns emerging for them that I had experienced. It was the shock of thinking they too would be suffering like I had. It was knowing I didn't have the energy to be the mother needed, or give them the love I knew would make the difference for them- This realisation was the catalyst for me. I knew I was not willing to do that to them.

My love for my daughters ignited a fire in me. Nothing would stand in my way after that.

Many of us have been brought up to not show our true feelings. We think being strong is not showing our true selves. So, we put out to the world the person we think we should be.

I believed that making my life better was pretending to be okay. Being like all the other people, who seemed to have life sussed. The problem was, deep down, no matter what I achieved I never believed I was like them. I never believed I was OK.

To run away from or mask our feelings never works out. Whatever we've buried remains buried unless we choose to bring it to light. Slowly I learned to gently allow stuck feelings to be felt. Allow my true beliefs to be seen and gently released. Gradually releasing the layers of stories- ones that feel dense and heavy.

Over time, when we are ready, we will step into the full magnificence of our TRUE nature. Under the layers of fear and hurt is where we truly reside.

Since the emergence of our species, fear is how we survived. We are the descendants of the wary folk. Our fight or flight reactions kept us alive. But we are moving into a new era, and this old way of being is no longer serving us.

When the amygdala is triggered, we move into our state of fight or flight- our reactive state. The areas of our brain that are creative or solve problems are no longer accessible. Our bodies change; they are alert, ready. Our breathing changes so we can react or run when danger strikes. This was important for our ancestors- it kept them alive. But many of us today live in this state; being triggered by things that are not dangerous to us. We just live in a state of anxiety because that's what we know. This has a huge effect on our health – physically, mentally and spiritually.

I'm not saying "I'm fixed" - This is about growth. I still mess up all the time, I regress, I am definitely a work in progress. But the key is the progress.

I'm writing this piece to tell you I didn't just survive.

At first it was just surviving, but I then learnt to cultivate something else.

How to really live, hope, wonder, trust. To feel my own strength and LOVE. Not the love that I searched for, but the love that's always present, inside- without us even consciously knowing about it at most times. The love that comes from within knows no limits. With a little space to grow, that love can be an ever-present source of nourishment; it heals us and overflows into the people we love and care for.

Whatever feelings we experience, whether they are pain, worry, discomfort or joy, peace and pleasure, each carries a message for us, guiding us back home. They may be clear and direct messages or may seem like an echo from a great distance. Each feeling carries its own frequency and lesson. They are the forgotten language that allows us to move forward into a new life- into freedom. I'm re-learning this language. I'm learning to listen and respond to my thoughts and feelings and to be there for myself. To trust.

A personal experience of moving from fear to love

Growing up with an awareness that a parent is unable to be there for you emotionally can lead to a toxic cycle. Blame and thoughts of the life that could have been, or the person I might have been took over. I felt anger for a very long time- stuck in my own perspective of my own situation.

As a teenager, I felt angry with the world. It felt shit. And things didn't get better as I grew older. The anxiety, feelings of hopelessness and complete overwhelm continued. I found life hard.

Despite the years of living with anxiety and depression, I never fully gave up on life getting better. I always kept trying. The problem was that it was fear that drove me to keep trying. Fear of things staying the same, or even getting worse. Fear of a future that seemed inevitable.

I'm lucky that I have always had a man in my life that has been there to light my path. For the first half of my life that man was my Dad. As a child, my beliefs that I was safe and that I was going to be ok were very much connected to the security I felt when I was with my Dad. He was always there for me and I knew how lucky I was for that.

Dad was fifty-five when I was born. A few members of my family that I loved very much died when I was five or six, and I developed a terrible fear of losing my Dad too. I couldn't imagine a life without him, but I was convinced I would soon lose him too.

From that point, I experienced a lot of years where my health and mental health deteriorated.

Amazingly, Dad kept going for a long time! In 2017 Dad was ninety-one, it was not long after I'd begun my spiritual journey.

So many opportunities were starting to open up in my life. I'd recently started my own business, I was pushing myself out of my comfort zone, doing online videos, striving to be better. After watching one of my videos, an old friend got in touch to tell me about the Hot Yoga studio in Sheffield, because she thought I'd like it. The day I called to ask them if I could come, they said they were doing a free taster session that evening.

I went and it was incredible! The people there were the most vibrant people I'd ever seen! They just looked so well and alive and I knew that was what I wanted too. From there, I began to discover Reiki and Energy Healing. My network of healers grew and grew.

Not long after I'd started going regularly, I went for a yoga session; it was a new teacher covering for someone that day. It was a really intense session in the heat. At the end, the teacher said we could send the energy we'd created to someone. My Dad had been very poorly so I decided to send it to him. In that moment, the experience I had was like my heart exploding. I suddenly felt the endless connection with my Dad, and I just knew that this love would go on forever. All the fear was all gone- it was beautiful. I just lay there, sobbing, as everyone else left the studio. I told my Dad the next day and he said he couldn't believe how he'd felt that night. He said he'd felt like superman! It made me laugh because when he used to work, they used to say "Is it a bird? Is it a plane? No! It's Cooper man!". I'm glad I'd helped him to feel like Cooper man again.

A few weeks later, my Dad passed. I felt so connected with him; I felt him with me. I'd feared this happening for so many years, and when it actually happened, it was the closest I'd felt to him since I was a child.

Since that time, I have practiced Meditation and Yoga Nidra daily. My journey brought me to a process, to release what I've kept inside; to return to alignment, to open to healing, peace and love.

Conscious Choice and Change

Everything is energy. Everything we see and feel. In our essence, we are simply energy. Our energy is fluid, alive, responsive. And our vibrational state determines the life creations we make in each moment. It shapes our experience and impacts the lives of those around us.

We are all creators. It's our nature to want things to be better and it's in our power to change things. But, if we live life looking for gratification from outside sources, we will only ever find temporary relief.

If we desire to truly change, then the change we desire can only really come by changing ourselves. Shaking up our energy and stepping into the unknown. Taking the leap and believing in ourselves - to surrender rather than push.

I see now the power of taking a step back. Of allowing a different perspective in. It sounds simple, but it takes courage to let go of the thing you've blamed and everything you've become dependent on.

I discovered I chose this experience- my family, my life- and there were reasons for my choice. With this awareness, my focus shifted. If these experiences were what I chose so I could learn, then what is it that they have taught me? What am I proud of? What am I not so proud of? What could I do better? These ways of approaching life instantly felt better.

Allowing in the wisdom that we have all come here with our own lessons and challenges will help us to view others in a new light too. Slowly, I've begun to allow myself to let go of the blame. To see people are who they are because of their own circumstances and journey. I am allowing myself to remember that maybe people are doing the best they are able to do, and maybe they mess things up, like I mess things up. Maybe someday, compassion, forgiveness and understanding will be my default.

This is also something I'm still working on.

Healing

Like a baby taking its first steps, when we begin to trust our inner guidance it's exhilarating and exciting! We get some momentum going, but then we fall. It takes time to learn to live in a completely new way- reprogramming all that we've known. We must learn to recognise the subconscious patterns, the limiting beliefs- that have usually been there for most of our lives- directing our choices, thoughts and actions. We must learn to show ourselves love and compassion.

Like a butterfly we slowly emerge as a new being.

So much of what we do comes from our subconscious programming. Up to about the age of seven we are like sponges, taking in the world around us and forming our views and beliefs.

When you have a parent who is deeply fearful, or angry, or apathetic- no matter how hard you fight it- their state will have had a great impact on you. When we don't build the connections in our brain in these early years, that we are safe and secure, the patterns of fear will most likely show up for the rest of our lives - unless we choose to address them.

WE ARE ABLE TO DO SOMETHING ABOUT THIS.

As soon as we accept the truth of our situation, accept our true selves- then we can help ourselves to change and grow.

One day
We accept we are here to grow
Growth feels like opening and ease
Feelings guiding us always.

When we are stuck in anger or resentment, we have a choice
To stay there
Believing the stories that keep us in that vibration
Or explore a new way to be
To see if we too are able to let go of the old stories and stuck-ness
And explore the landscape of a new life that can unfold before us
if we allow it to.
Step by step we go.

I see now, how my life has a purpose- and that purpose is growth! We can feel the energy of this choice, learn which choices are helping us to grow and move forward on our path- and which are not.

When we shift our energy into higher states, we allow ourselves to move forward, flowing with life. We can then learn in states of enjoyment, rather than through suffering.

Looking back with kindness
I looked back on choices I made and judged her
She was broken
It was all wrong

But for every other soul I saw their journey
Their inner beauty, their effort.
I had no idea that every time I saw the light in others, I was seeing me.
Every journey has been part of getting us here.

Love, Expansion

To heal, to transition- takes time.

The balance between our outer life and inner life may need to change. We know this, when we listen and feel.

I began to spend many more hours resting, meditating. My body told me to and I answered its call. Usually, between five and half five in the morning, when it was peaceful. It all came flowing- peace, ease that I'd never experienced before, feelings of connection, healing, love and comfort.

I am so grateful to be experiencing this, in this lifetime.

Love is timeless. Every time we've felt lost, we have the power to return - to remember. To travel to the times we needed love and be there for ourselves. To provide them with the comfort they needed.

Love, heal and move on. You feel the shift. The energy that restricted your breath- free-er, your body- finally moving.

For the first time I feel proud of myself; I feel hopeful.

Hope for the future is a truly precious gift.

Marie Batty lives with her husband, Robin and 2 daughters; Martha and Edie. She's made Sheffield her home for the past 19 years since moving up from Leicester.

Marie is passionate about sharing what she's learnt on her journey so far- from feeling defined by depression and chronic illness, to a life that feels good.

Her lifelong dream of becoming a published author has become a reality with the publication of this book. She's now looking forward to writing in greater detail about returning to a life of balance, and sharing the many strategies and techniques that she's learnt along the way.

She is currently sharing workshops to help women heal their inner wounds.

Contact Marie at: Bernadettebatty@gmail.com

Believe in your Power
Melissa Watson

I have been on an intense healing journey for the past three years. I have been through my share of trauma and made many mistakes thanks to it - only causing myself more trauma and pain. I wanted to get off the merry-go-round of cyclical trauma. I knew I needed some deep healing, but I didn't know where to look. I knew nothing. Although working with therapists had played an important role, I needed more, something else. The Universe helped me out, by introducing me to The Law of Attraction through synchronicities. This theory posits that like attracts like and that thoughts become things; that our thoughts are energy that interact with The Universe. When I learned about this, I started to become aware of my thoughts. To my surprise, they were mostly negative. I was riddled with limiting beliefs that played out throughout the day in the back of my head. Thoughts that I wasn't enough, that I wasn't loveable, that I was broken. "If only I were smarter, prettier, skinnier, more successful, more accomplished, then I'd be good enough for x, y, z."

I set out to change my thoughts, by changing my limiting beliefs. I used every force known to woman - meditation, nutrition, exercise, gratitude, positive affirmations, cold showers for discipline, Epsom salt baths, journaling, walks in nature, yoga, listening to motivational podcasts, reading self-development books. I devoted my days to healing and I came at it from every angle. I created a vision board, a way to tell myself and The Universe what I wanted to manifest in my life: love, more time for yoga, adventures like canoeing and kayaking, entrepreneurship, empowering women, writing, dance, acting and so much more!

Through my healing journey, I discovered energy healing. I found it helped me release emotions and trauma that I'd been holding onto without even realizing it. It even helped me heal from long Covid. I decided to become a Reiki Master because I wanted to share this form of healing with everyone I could.

So many of those things on my vision board have come to fruition - often, to my delight, serendipitously. I am currently writing a book to help empower women. I started my own business, Envisioned Life Institute LLC. I am a Trauma-Healing and Life Purpose Embodiment Coach. I want to help others who are going through a similar situation as I was; to introduce them to these forms of healing so they can step into their most joyful and aligned selves to live their dream.

I was recently visited over a dozen times by a hummingbird that brought me the idea to study Shamanism. I want to be more connected to nature, to The Universe, to everything. I want to build my practice spiritually as I continue my spiritual growth.

If you are a little lost today, I urge you to listen to your inner voice. Listen to The Universe, as it is speaking to you - you just must listen. Take time to heal. I suggest building a gratitude practice and working on forgiveness of yourself and others. Use journaling to discover your own limiting beliefs. Use meditation, yoga, and positive affirmations to turn those limiting beliefs into empowering beliefs about yourself and the world. Consider trying Reiki energy healing to remove blocks in your chakras, so you can release past traumas and negative emotions that are holding you back. Remember that you are powerful beyond words, you just have to believe it.

IG/FB @envisionedlifeinstitute
www.envisionedlifeinstitute.com

We Never Walk Alone
Shyma Jundi

Have you ever had a moment in which you're transported back in time? It can be a sensory experience, like a piece of music or a memorable scent – or sometimes it can even be a certain phrase, or the way a person talks or laughs. And boom – a memory comes knocking, clear as day.

Sometimes these are happy memories and that's great. It can lead to awkward moments of giggling in the dentist's chair, or trying not to laugh in the middle of a Zoom meeting- but in the grand scheme of things it's all good. But sometimes, the memory is less fun. It's something you thought you'd processed. Something you may have gone to therapy for, and it may have taken place years ago. You instantly start beating yourself up, thinking "come on, don't be affected by this. We've processed this, we've done the work. Don't react. You're going backwards".

I've been through these moments, countless times. They're unpredictable, in terms of when they'll come, and when they'll go. When you're with other people, and trying to have a good time, they can hit like a bullet – you don't want to step away to process, and yet somehow, you're not fully present anymore. The jokes people are telling don't seem funny, and the small talk you're making is feeling exhausting.

The jarring flashbacks can be from an experience from many years ago. For me, they often remind me of a period of my life which actually started like a dream. I'd applied to a major company, for a unique role that wasn't normally advertised. It was an intense application process and I went through many interview stages, not knowing if I was going to make it to the next. But somehow, I did. It was a moment of total relief and elation when I received a phone call, informing me they were going to make me a job offer.

I swallowed my nerves, gathered my strength and walked into their flashy offices. It wasn't the best of starts – I forgot to bring my passport to the induction day and had to travel back home to get it. But I made it through, and met my new team. And that's when my awakening journey started to begin – and unravel – simultaneously. Little did I know that when I'd asked for a challenge, it was about to be delivered in spades.

The first few weeks were fine, though I noted how odd some of the behaviours were. Everyone always seemed rushed and harassed, even when things could have been handled calmly. There was an obsession with giving 'feedback' -even feedback about a five-minute chat. And then the critical comments started coming in. At the beginning they didn't feel too bad – I was told to check in more with the team while working on tasks, and to arrive at the office really early each morning, to show how keen I was. But they became increasingly intrusive, where everything from how I dressed to how I spoke was analysed. I became more and more disillusioned, and the exhaustion of dealing with it meant I had depleted energy to actually focus on the work. I thought I could get away with working in a more lethargic way, but was quickly pulled aside by the director.

"I need TWICE as much from you", she concluded, after giving me a humiliating dressing down. In that moment I made a choice – I remember telling myself to put on an alter ego when I pulled my work pass over my neck every morning – to stop being Shyma and instead become Amber – a super confident and motivated worker who could walk onto the office floor like she owned it. It was that, or leave. And I wasn't prepared to quit yet. But playing a persona lasted about a week before I felt like I was going to burnout. Taking on an alter ego is fine in bursts (think of Beyonce and Sasha Fierce), but living it all day every day is just inauthentic and unsustainable.

Unsurprisingly, I was pulled aside by my director again. "You look really stressed when you're here", she said, sternly. "And then when I see you leaving in the evening, you look really happy and relaxed". I froze, as I always did when she was giving me a telling off. I keenly searched for the perfect response that would quell her anger – it didn't come. I settled for nodding, silently, which just seemed to infuriate her even more. "I find these conversations awkward", she said pointedly. "Me too", I thought silently, wishing she would stop initiating them.

I've always feared criticism, and this situation forced me to face this fear big time. Before this job, I'd done a lot of inner work on my relationship with criticism. I'd integrated the belief that the opinions of others are their own perceptions of the world – and not a reflection on me. This belief had been bringing me much peace. But it was now being challenged to the hilt, as I was told countless times that it was, indeed, me who was lacking.

I started job hunting – I was desperate to escape the overwhelming stress of an environment where I was literally judged for how I sat (I received 'feedback' to say that bending over my laptop screen looked unprofessional). I felt like I couldn't breathe. I used to try and book desks away from the team and the director – I viewed her like a wild animal to be scared of, and if I saw her in the office I'd try and hide, or walk a long route round the building so I didn't encounter her.

The day it ended was the day I breathed the biggest sigh of relief. I packed up my belongings, shredded all my paperwork and left, feeling so free. I hadn't secured another job, so it was a tense few months afterwards to find my next gig. When I found it, even though it was worlds apart from my negative experience, I still brought so much of that fear with me. I worked on tenterhooks a lot of the time, trying to avoid being criticised. I worked intense hours for the first couple of weeks until I looked up from my laptop, late in the evening, and realised everyone had left and I was the only one still there. I was surprised anytime anyone seemed happy with my work or gave me a compliment; and I worried about whether it was just a moment in time, and the criticism and complaints were just around the corner.

It's been a long journey to process the fallout from that traumatic place, and to an extent I'm still processing it now. The lesson is deep – un-entwining worth from performance. Realising that sometimes it is the case of not being able to persuade a monkey that honey is sweeter than a banana. I'm still the same person – yes maybe a bit older and wiser now, but the essence is still the same. And yet, for some people, that was never going to be enough – even when I dressed like they wanted, came in for the hours they wanted, and tried to adopt the persona they wanted.

My awakening journey is coming to realise that my worth isn't tied to the external. I read Human Design Charts as part of my business – part of Human Design is identifying whether your inner energetic centres are open or closed, which helps create your personal body graph (like an energetic blueprint). I have an open heart centre, which means that I am always seeking external validation of my worth – I struggle with knowing that my worth is inherent. If it's something you struggle with too, please take time to reflect on moments when you weren't enough in one situation, and yet were more than enough in another. It just goes to show you that worth is a decision you make – not something you need 'feedback' on.

I love manifestation, and as a learner and teacher of manifestation, my understanding of it over the years has evolved and deepened. And sometimes the path of least resistance is to change the environment that is bringing you so much pain. Many manifestation teachers speak of changing your inner world to shift the outer world – even in very unpreferred circumstances. And whilst I don't deny that's a possible approach (assuming of course the circumstances don't involve abuse of any kind), the utter stress and heartache that one can endure, trying to change our experience instead of admitting that we would be recognised somewhere else, can be unbearable. So never believe that your lot is your lot, and that if you change your environment, you won't change your experience. It took a couple of changes in jobs before I finally felt like I could thrive in confidence. I still get Imposter Syndrome, and I still fear being told off and not being good enough. But over the years of therapy and coaching, I'm beginning to learn that what I'm really fearing is my own judgement. If I knew without a shadow of a doubt that I would never abandon myself emotionally, and that the opinions of others is not something I need to internalise, I think my fear of judgement would melt away. So that's the path I'm navigating.

If you're on a manifestation journey, on the surface it may seem like you want to experience a 'thing' – whether that thing is a soulmate, huge abundance, the great career, a flourishing business, impeccable health etc. But through the journey, particularly in the areas which seem to be tougher for you, you'll see that the challenges are serving to bring you closer to yourself and closer to Source. I was asked recently whether I could trust that Source would fulfil all my desires. I hesitated – questioning whether my desires were worthy enough to be granted, knowing that in the past that things that I've wanted e.g., that corporate job, turned out to be so painful. And it's in that hesitation that I realised 'this is the point'. Yes, I'd love to manifest the stuff, but where is that going to get me – fear of losing the stuff? If I lean into trust, if I can deepen my relationship with Source, that's where the real peace resides. Not all manifestation teachings emphasise this – it doesn't always feel as sexy as the lure of more immediate results e.g., the 'manifest £5k in 5 days' style of message. So, if there's something you've been manifesting for a while and it hasn't materialised yet, I invite you to question whether there's a deeper lesson for you to learn. And to reflect on how you are being served by the unfolding of that lesson.

Realising your worth is inherent is not an overnight job, and you may, like me, take a few steps forward and then have wobbles. Being gentle with yourself is part of the journey. I fully recommend surrounding yourself with people who can remind you of how incredible you are, especially when you may not be feeling it yourself. They don't have to do this by explicitly telling you (though that can work great!) - sometimes it will be in the wide smile that crosses their face when they see you walk into the room, or the affection in their voice when they say your name, or the joke they make about a funny encounter you had together. It's most important for us, ourselves, to see and feel our worth- but our loved ones can be vital in guiding us back to that when we get a little lost. And asking for support, whether it's from loved ones or from professional Therapists or Coaches, can be instrumental. You'll need different types of support at different times of your journey – sometimes I ask my mentors for multiple calls a month, and sometimes I can go for months where I feel settled. Reading this book will hopefully bring you solace in knowing that we all go through awakening journeys, and even though our journeys are individual, when we share and open up about them, we never walk alone.

Shyma's own awakening journey has equipped her with tools and techniques that she loves to share with others. She works one to one with women to empower them with unshakeable self-love, self-belief, and a supercharged ability to manifest a life of their dreams.

Using techniques such as Emotional Freedom Tapping (EFT), she helps women release the resistance they may have, so they can attract their desires with ease.

Contact
Instagram @shymajundi
Email info@shymajundi.com

Her Price
Swey Jitti

They say, they say
What a beauty it is
To be, to hold
A woman

Yet I hear them think
As they try to sink their teeth
In flesh so pink
It's cruel

So she roared in rage
Dared them to get close
"You see, dear men
I'm no human"

In fear they screamed
Their egos bruised with guilt
The shame of hurting
A queen

So they cursed her name
Set her frame to flame
A sight so sour
So cruel...

The price she paid
As a woman, we say
Is the burn of the greed
By men of no use; By men
Who refused to see truth

So there her vessel lay,
Returning to the earth
For even though, her worth was tallied
By men who knew less

Her wisdom, her truth, her vision
So invaluable, so delicate, so full
That she lived on
In ways they'd never know

For infinite,
was a word too small
To carry the weight
of her soul.
Swey Jitti
https://linkpop.com/sweyjitti

Mujer Sabia (Wise Woman)
Tania Ferreyra

To my darling daughter,

My body is making its unavoidable, inevitable, human female journey along the river of life. It began at source, in the bright and pure springs of childhood; bubbling into the valleys and rolling waters of puberty, before cascading into the deep roar and rush of early womanhood. For a while, a brief and unexpected confluence of love and attraction resulted in me swirling, unexpectedly - brutally - magically, into Motherhood, where, for a time, I did not know which way was up. But I survived - and you, my darling- you *thrived*. Loving you brought calm and clear waters, and a fierce love I had never known before. Yet, before I began to realise, the river had already started carrying me on, into dark and wide Valleys, where the churning and turbulent waters of perimenopause flow.

It is here that I am treading water; attempting to regain my breath and composure, before continuing my way along the river. There are, I know, many more twists and turns to face. Unknown and un-navigated, until such a time that I eventually reach the peace and wide-open arms of the sea.

My beautiful girl, you are like a miracle to me every day. You are the embodiment of my wish to be a loving and protective presence, teacher, guide and friend. You are now at the age I was when difficult and painful things were happening in my life, and this is such a healing place for me to be. Thank you for this opportunity, this blessing, to now see the world through *your* eyes. It is my privilege and honour to be here alongside you.

You are so gloriously and magnificently yourself. Comfortable in your own skin. I witness you living wild and free, with no fear of judgement or control; safe to express yourself, to be whatever you feel, knowing that every single part of you is welcome and loved.

My story so far has been rich and ripe and with pleasure, pain, laughter, fear, disappointment, love, tears, loss and learning.

As a girl, I was solitary, with few friends. Nature and animals were my medicine and peace. I would often roam the countryside, talking to the birds, horses and cattle in the fields. Along my walks, I would linger beneath Oak and Birch trees, wrapping my arms tightly around their strong trunks- feeling a peace and protection which was absent from my life. I would lie in fields of tall grass, and, hidden from everything but the open sky, would let my tears spill out as I whispered my secrets down into Mother Earth.

I felt like I never *belonged* - not within my own home, nor in the small English village where I had ended up. At a young age my own Mother had fled with me from my homeland, leaving the crumbling instability of her marriage and the country's politics tens of thousands of miles away.

In this new world, my black hair and brown skin attracted unwanted stares, whispers and unwelcome comments. Grown adults, through fear and ignorance, taught their own children to be afraid and hostile towards me - a small, quiet girl who wanted nothing but love and acceptance.

Time passed, and I grew into a tall and striking young woman. Now even more visible, I did *everything* possible to blend in, to hide my difference. I stayed out of the sun for fear of becoming more tanned. I bleached my hair and my skin, changed my accent, pretended to like the music and the fashion the other girls followed and tried my very best to give a convincing act that I was as attracted to the local boys as they were to me. If only they had known that I liked to read books and to write poetry, play my guitar, draw, paint and dance!

Day by day, year after year, I hid my true identity deep inside- pushing it down into my bones and my body and my big, beautiful, broken heart. I deliberately stopped taking notice; disconnecting from nature and the things that I once loved. Numbing my mind and body with poisons, which deadened and blurred me. I busied myself with toxic, ego driven people- setting aside my own hopes and dreams, as I placed my time and energy into their dramas and needs. I slowly became lost to myself.

Eventually - unsurprisingly, I cracked apart for the first time. I felt the darkness approaching like a storm - saw it rolling in, thunderous, dark and furious. For so many years I fell in and out of the dark. I truly learnt who was genuine, as friends and even family fell away.

Despite trying to find it, there was no magic cure. Healing only came when, after going back to the dark over and over again, I eventually began to listen to *myself*, to my own inner voice- realising it had been there all along. I had just stopped listening.

I grew to understand that I only had myself to lean on, that nothing externally could provide me with the care and love I could and should give to myself. Despite the pain, cracking open had ultimately let the dark out and the light in. And so slowly, I began my awakening. It became a process of *remembering* who I was and why I was here, whilst at the same time learning to forget who I was not and letting go of the stories that kept me from my full power.

So, my precious girl - some wisdoms:

- Live a life of awareness- observe and notice. I wish I could prevent it, but, if you experience pain, choose not to look back in anger, or forward in fear - but around in awareness. Each experience - good and bad, offers up wisdom.

- Wake early each morning; in time to see the dawn, when the world is hushed, still and asleep. It is pure magic. The stillness of this time will remain with you throughout your day. During these precious hours, meditate and journal. Set intentions for your day ahead.

- There is such value in keeping a journal. Pour your thoughts, ideas and drawings onto each page. Press flowers and grasses between its pages. In time, when you look back, your journal will enable you to reflect upon and better understand your life. It will show you what you did the same, what you did differently, and help you to see patterns and challenges you would not have seen otherwise. It will help you to write your own roadmap.

- Always, always, be yourself. Don't buy into the idea of perfection. Embrace mess, disorder, imperfection and chaos! Nobody ends up living the life they expect or dream of. It is utterly exhausting and futile, to want a perfect home, a perfect, face, perfect body. Perfectionism is an illusion. You will never, ever, attain perfection and happiness at the same time. Do not waste your time trying.

- Please love Pacha Mama right. She has been terribly hurt and abused for so long. Do what you can to tread lightly upon her; help her to heal. She holds the answers and is our medicine and our meditation. Every day, get out and walk in nature and commune with the trees, plants, animals, around you. They will be your teachers. Ground yourself. Take off your shoes and walk on the earth. Lie on the ground and look up at the sky. Close your eyes and listen to the music nature makes.

- Start a Garden. Work with the light of the sun and the moon to grow flowers, trees, fruit and vegetables. Water and talk to them, watch them progress through the year. Love them right and they will reward you in abundance.

- Save the Bees.

- Practice mantras and affirmations. There are thousands of powerful, beautiful mantras which have immense power to reset our brains. Affirmations remind us that there is such strength to be found in the words we choose to say, and repeat. Two small words, - "I am" - followed by a kind or positive adjective ("I am...bold...brave...strong...I am e*nough)* are so simple, but so effective.

- Learn about the sheer magnificence, perfection and miracle of your female human body. Honour it. It is yours to keep and yours to give; let it always be in the pursuit of your own learning, pleasure or love.

- Never, ever, change yourself for anybody, or to try and fit in. You are a shining, perfect soul. If you are uniquely and unashamedly yourself, you will find your tribe- the people like you. Be so purely you, doing your own thing and dancing to your own song, that people will naturally be drawn to you.

- Embody Sensuality. Touch your skin, your curves. Look at yourself in the mirror. Love the unique colour of your skin, eyes, hair. Know each curve and crevice, each toe and finger. Every line and scar. They all tell the story of you.

- Decorate and adorn yourself. Worship you. If you feel, tattoo your body with beautiful and meaningful images - your body is your canvas.

- Choose beautiful clothes - they don't need to be new or expensive. And there is so much joy to be found in thrift and charity shops, which have the added bonus of giving back to others.

- Other times, hide away in your oldest, softest clothes, and spend time doing nothing. The times we take to restore are just as important as the time we take to be seen in all our sensuality.

- Attend to your body - feed, water, nourish and nurture it and it will repay you with strength and good health. Practise Yoga. Walk. Swim.

- Understand the cycles of the Moon, Sun and seasons. Apply this same knowledge to your relationships, to the way you live your life. Everything is about lifecycles and has a natural beginning, middle and end- which will repeat over and over. Reinvent and recreate yourself with each changing season. It is a gift.

- Forgive. Remember that your feelings and thoughts do not define you. If at times, you cannot forgive, release. Take yourself to an outdoor space and place your bare feet and hands on the ground. Sink your fingers and toes into the soil and imagine those feelings and experiences flowing out of you, dark and dense, into the earth- where they will dissipate.

- Observe yourself in difficult situations. Get curious. The truth is, we don't respond to what happens; we respond to our *perception* of what happens. We can't control the world, but we can control our reaction to it.

- Salt water, sweat and tears heal. Go to the sea as often as possible - It is a magnificent and powerful reminder of our smallness. Dance with passion and abandon - either alone or close to others. Cry whenever you feel the tears rise up within you. Allow them to cleanse and calm you.

- Remember to have fun! Don't take life so seriously. Be silly. Remember and honour the child which will always exist within you.

- Create and stick to healthy boundaries. Alcohol, drugs, fear and sexual attraction will mess with your boundaries, so be mindful.

- Create! Paint, draw, write, dance, sing, knit, sew, without self-judgement or focusing on achieving perfection. Get out of the way and let creativity move through you. Your hands and voice will create such beauty.

- Meditate. Make it a daily practice. It helps us to cope with the human experience; allowing us to observe and acknowledge our thoughts, and to then let them go. It invites stillness into your mind and body. Think of it as letting the mud in our minds settle, clearing the surface. We are spiritual beings; we live within ourselves. Meditation allows us to connect with our Soul, to touch infinity.

- Learn how to Breathe properly. Once discovered, it will transform your life. The only thing that stays with you throughout your life is your beautiful breath. It is the foundation of life, yet we take it for granted. When you can manage your breath properly, you can cope with any situation in life. The right breath can reset, re-regulate, energise or relax you. Throughout the day, make time to focus upon inhaling gratitude, and exhaling thanks to your breath for always being there.

- Introduce ritual and the sacred into your life and practice them consistently. Ritual is the way we make something invisible, visible; turning a feeling or an intention into symbolic form, making it tangible, touchable. See the sacred in yourself. It is not as esoteric as it appears. It is a feeling within you, not a thing. The sacred is what we *are*, not what we *do.* In the smallest moments, as you go about your daily life, you can connect to, and practice the sacred, through ritual. It's as simple as lighting a candle, incense or burning herbs, setting an intention as you make a perfect cup of coffee or a beautiful meal, each step prepared with love and purpose. Sitting with and connecting with the spirit of nature, plants or animals is a fast and direct way to access moments of the sacred.

- Look for the good in everything. It is a beautiful world, full of love and joy.

- With love and a prayer, let go of people and situations which don't align with you and your soul's purpose.

- Do the right thing. Call out bullying and injustice. Cross the road to help someone. Pick the bee up from the pavement. You will be them and they will be you in future incarnations.

- Honour your heritage and your ancestors. Create a beautiful altar where you can place photographs of the family, a small sprig of fresh flowers and a candle. They will sigh their thanks.

- That thing that you think is your weakness is actually your light. It is also your teacher. Sit with it and ask it what it is trying to show you.

- Check in with yourself as often as possible. The body holds such wisdom. It is as simple as closing your eyes, scanning your body, feeling for any sensations in your body, noticing any tension or irritation. Massages, salt baths, swimming, exercise, will all help you to release and regulate how you feel within yourself.

- Trust and listen to your gut instinct. It *never* lies.

- Practice an attitude of gratitude every single day. Look at what you *have*; not what you don't have, or what's happened to you. There is always something to be grateful for. Being grateful raises your frequency and your energy.

- Approach others in the spirit of love and acceptance, with no agenda. Be humble and sincere. Ask how you can help. Be of service.

I am so sorry, but in your life, there will be times when you feel lost and afraid. When I cannot be there, when you feel the world is just too much - when you need answers to questions, or you feel lost, regretful, disappointed or sad. When nothing is known with any certainty, close your eyes, my beautiful girl. Place your hands over your heart and womb and sigh deeply into yourself, asking your heart to reveal its wisdom to you. If you listen, the wisdom is there. I promise.

Know always and forever that I love you. One day you will be a wise woman too.

Mama.
x

Tania is an Argentinian Writer and Playwright, Kundalini Yoga Teacher, Reiki Healer and Curandera- with a special interest in working to support and heal Women who have experienced trauma. She runs and facilitates workshops, retreats and circles at her magical and secluded Ashram in North Wales. In this special collaboration, Tania shares a letter of awakening and wisdom written for her daughter.

For enquiries contact: hola@taniaferreyra.com

She Sat in All Her Wonder
Jo Cantle

She sat in all her wonder
And pondered who was she
That God would place within her
A light for all to see

A light so bright and golden
A light so proud to be
She sat in all her wonder
And asked God "Who was she?"

To be given such an awesome gift
A gift so light and free
She sat in all her wonder
And asked God "What will be?"

"If I am to shine this light,
And dare to act as me,
Will you be there to catch me
Will you be there to see?"

So God replied with kindness
And God replied with glee
"My child, I made you glorious,
I made you just like me."

"I made you so your light can shine,
So all the world can see,
That everyone has this gift inside,
The secret to be free."

"The love that waits inside of them
The feeling that is key
My love in all its glory
A love that's really me."

So, she sat in wonder
And asked God "Who are we?"
He said "You are my Children,
And you are part of me."

"Your soul is love manifested
Your body a physical realm
And you walk in glory
With my calling at the helm."

"My child, your light is beaming
Let go of the hurt of the past,
Because I am here to guide you,
My love will always last."

The girl she sat in wonder
And pondered all she could be
When she felt the love within her
She realised "I am free!"

Jo Cantle
linktr.ee/feelgoodforyoucoach

The Divine Collective

The Divine Collective publishes conscious messages to uplift and inspire. We are passionate about providing a platform for those who wish to express their soul voice. Our mission is to provide opportunities for those wishing to share their written voice. We help them to express authentically and to connect with resonant souls. We do this through book collaborations, Author mentorship, writing workshops and poetry events.

To find out more please visit:
www.divinecollectivepublishing.net/
thedivinecollective

And follow us on our socials:

Instagram: @thedivinecollectivepublishing

Facebook: The Divine Collective

Printed in Great Britain
by Amazon

12191407R00169